MW01452257

Sleepwalker

SLEEPWALKER

Michael Cadnum

St. Martin's Press
New York

SLEEPWALKER. Copyright © 1991 by Michael Cadnum. All rights reserved. Printed in the United States of America. No part of this book may be used or reproduced in any manner whatsoever without written permission except in the case of brief quotation embodied in critical articles or reviews. For information, address St. Martin's Press, 175 Fifth Avenue, New York, N.Y. 10010.

Design by Amelia R. Mayone

Library of Congress Cataloging-in-Publication Data

Cadnum, Michael.
    Sleepwalker / Michael Cadnum.
       p.   cm.
    ISBN 0-312-04995-1
    I. Title.
PS3553.A314S55 1991
813'.54—dc20
                                                                                      90-48525
                                                                                          CIP

for Sherina

As I did stand my watch upon the hill,
I look'd toward Birnam, and anon methought
The wood began to move.

—Macbeth, V.v

Sleepwalker

Prologue

She was walking on the water.
She was walking toward him across the surface of the lake, and even though he knew he couldn't do it he found himself stepping onto the water.
The wrinkling of the water beneath his feet was like pleasure, but all he could think was, She's dead.
She's dead—this can't be happening.
He struggled to wake, and he couldn't. She was drifting toward him, and getting closer, and he did not want to see her. The dream had him, a grip he could not escape.
Until at last he was awake, cold with sweat.
He was standing in the middle of the bedroom, trembling.
In my sleep, he thought. I got out of my bed in my sleep, and began walking toward her.
Perhaps, he wondered, this is how it begins. This is how it is, when you lose your mind.

In the nights that followed, he would wake and find himself standing in one of the darkened rooms of his apartment. He would find himself with a shirt half buttoned, his running shoes in his hand. Once he found himself in the suit he had bought in Paris, his tie in his hand, as though he had been attending a party and had been overcome by drink.

He would find books tugged from the shelf, and once found a kitchen drawer in the middle of the living room, napkins and plastic roll undisturbed.

He was afraid.

At first he could tolerate it. He was revising a series of lectures for an upcoming book. His articles continued to be published, and international telephone calls continued to congratulate him on one book or another. Colleagues continued to be kind, putting a hand on his shoulder, inviting him to the sort of party in which people talk more than drink. Dr. Wilson invited him into his office for that wink-and-only-we-will-know bourbon from time to time, and told him that if there was anything he could do. . . . And of course there never was.

But then the dream began to change.

One night she walked toward him across the blue water, the fragments of light reflected over her body, and he remembered how he loved her, and that he could never see her again. And then he saw, as she grew closer, that she was not alive, that her skin was gray and brittle as ash, and that as she smiled the flakes of skin fell away, fluttering like butterflies, and gradually exposed her charred skull.

He woke, gasping.

He stood under the eucalyptus trees. It was dark, and the freeway hissed in the distance. Headlights sliced past. The twelve-story condominium loomed, a strip of lights marking the elevators at the end of each hall. The wind lifted the leaves in the trees. The air was damp. It was nearly always damp here beside San Francisco Bay. He breathed fog, the faint tang of eucalyptus, and the faintest soil of carair.

He was nearly glad to be there, eucalyptus seeds under his feet, those bell-shaped, molar-sized seeds, and then it was the feel of those seeds under his feet that made him wonder. His feet were too sensitive. Too aware of not only the seeds, but the dirt. One toe rested in a twig—he could feel it distinctly under his big toe.

He looked down.

He was naked. He fell to a crouch, huddling. Bare. He shivered, although it was not so cold. And not really so dark. There was

2

too much light at night, he realized. San Francisco spilled a bronze glow into its low clouds, the Bay Bridge hulked, glittering, and a truck rumbled by on the freeway defined by the amber lights at its corners. Davis's shadow crouched before him.

Light, everywhere. And he was naked. Completely. Stark. He scurried to a tree, and then cringed. There was poison oak here on Albany Hill. A dose of poison oak would last for weeks. He was in trouble—in very bad trouble—and he sank to his knees in an effort to calm himself, and gave a jump as a pebble bit into his knee.

He laughed, a short cough. Davis Lowry, internationally respected for his intellect, and even, he had to admit, his looks—distinguished, much honored Professor Lowry—was naked behind a tree, and all the doors back to his apartment on the twelfth floor, including the doors to the lobby, were locked. The building was patrolled by phlegmatic but no doubt sleepless security guards. He found himself holding his breath and counting the floors—twelve of them before he could reach his apartment with the wonderful view, all the way at the top.

He scrabbled in the half dark and found a short claw of dead leaves he dangled before his most crucial nakedness, and he sidled a few steps. He could not guess what time it was. But if dawn began to barely glow, he was finished. He let the bunch of dead leaves fall. They would be useless.

Don't panic, he whispered to himself. Be still. You need a plan.

Fine, a plan. That would be easy. He would walk—stroll, saunter—all the way around the building, wave at the security guard, punch his code into the buttons at the traffic gate, and wander in, like a man just back from taking the night air.

He could wait at a side door, huddled behind the pot of azaleas, and hope that an early riser, or someone with a dachshund with a weak bladder, decided to go for a walk. Someone with a healthy heart, not one of the more trembly, blinky women who always looked up with anxiety even in normal times, even when he was waiting for an elevator, carrying his Florentine-leather briefcase. He felt sorry for them. There were dozens of timid older women. He was sure that the sight of him now would give them a stroke.

He could wait at the automatic gate, a shuddering metal cage that lifted, held itself open, and then fell. If a car engine died the gate would slowly fall onto the car while the driver cursed. The gate was deliberate and slow. That was what mattered now. Slow. He

3

could dart in, like a very large, hairless cat. He was in fairly good shape—not that he wanted this much of his physique to be illuminated by the stumpy lights around the periphery of the junipers. He could run from where he was to the garage before the gate groaned shut. But as he crouched, chewing his thumbnail, it was plain that this was one night on which everyone was home, and no one was going for a drive. No one. Everyone was asleep.

It was a long wait for nothing. Time was being wasted. Day was coming. He could feel the earth rolling like a great stone eye, and hundreds of people in the very building before him were groaning awake beside chirping alarm clocks. He had no time. He had to do something—now.

He trotted to the chain-link fence, hooked his toes into it, scrambled over it, and fell to the other side. But it was good to be doing something. Wonderful to be taking some action.

A door opened, and light spilled. He froze, and scrambled, with more discomfort than he had anticipated, behind a black azalea bush.

A dog panted. A woman huddled in an overcoat was tugged along by a basset hound. The dog squatted beside a drain grid in the concrete, well trained or naturally considerate. The door shut halfway and paused, a wedge of light, and he nearly leaped for it, but then, just as he gathered himself, the door sighed and closed, except for a slit of yellow.

It clicked shut.

He prepared a statement in his mind. "Forgive me, but I have been—" What could he say? Taken by spirits? Undressed by supernatural forces? He said nothing. The woman and her dog continued out a gate and up the hill, and this was bad. This meant that it was not a midnight emergency. It was a predawn walk. Night was nearly done.

He ran, hunched over, feeling the way he thought a beast must feel, a furtive dog, a feral cat. Or worse—a werewolf, just returning from the slaughter and not yet fully human. He slid into the darkest shade, the canyon of night beside the wall, and thought, Perhaps I have done something. He spread his fingers before his eyes. He couldn't be sure. Perhaps there was blood.

But this was childish. Someday this would all be an amusing story. He would entertain his friends over port and Stilton. Yes, that funny time, he would laugh, when I was naked.

4

He crept, scrambled, hesitated. He peered around a corner, and then took several long, slow breaths. He padded down cold, stone slabs, rosemary bushes scratching his ankles.

The security guards' office, a cubicle of black glass, reflected his black silhouette. He cleared his throat, and shivered, because now it was cold in the wind from the Bay. And it was more than cold. Some day, he consoled himself again, he would look back at this. Some day he would tell it—a funny story. His mouth was glue. His pulse fluttered in his throat.

He tapped on the glass.

He tapped again.

The glass window slid open, and a jowly profile glanced out in the wrong direction.

"I'm here," said Davis. "I'm naked," he added, so the guard might be somewhat prepared, and also so the guard would know that Davis was not intoxicated or experimenting with drugs. "I walk in my sleep," he offered.

The man vanished.

It had seemed like a good plan, thought Davis, gazing at the black glass of the guard booth. He had done the best he could.

The guard hurried from a door, and swept a woolly, pleasingly scratchy blanket around Davis's shoulders, around all of him.

He overdressed that day, wearing a sweater under his tweed jacket, and even sported a snap-brim hat he had bought years before, in an attempt to look like someone in a *Thin Man* movie. He was too hot, but he took nothing off.

He bought a pair of pajamas, and fastened them with safety pins that night. Surely he would prick a finger, he thought, if he tried to strip at two A.M. He propped chairs against his door and around his bed, so that he would have to climb over them to get out of bed at all. He put dictionaries and medical encyclopedias in awkward places, so that even fully awake, after brushing his teeth, he stubbed his toe and danced on one foot for a moment. This was a good sign. All would be well.

He ran four miles before dinner. He ate a lamb chop and steamed rice, boring, digestible. After dinner he drove to the track and walked another three miles. When he sat in the darkness, relaxing on the empty bleachers, he knew that on this night he would sleep well.

He yawned before the television, and drank one beer. He felt quiet inside, weary and complete. He took a long, hot shower. By then, his legs were stone and his eyes burned. He yawned great sleepy-lion yawns. He pinned himself into his pajamas and fumbled for the radio alarm, because, as sleepy as he was, he knew that he might sleep until noon the next day unless something woke him.

He pulled the blankets up to his chin.

And then he missed her. He missed her as he had missed her every night for the last six months. This time, though, it was especially bad. His grief was a physical pain. He reached to the empty place in the bed and, after a long time, he slept.

She walked toward him, again, across the lake.

He was in an amazing place. He knew, though, that it was not a dream. The wind was cool, and the radio tower across the black bay was a single prick of light that pulsed off and on. The Golden Gate Bridge was a necklace of light. There was the swimming pool far below, and the tennis courts. The wind smoothed back his hair, and he spread his arms.

This was where he lived, yet he had never seen it like this. An airplane, a tiny, blinking jewel, floated across the sky, and only then did he sense his bare feet. His feet gripped a narrow, hard shelf. A board, perhaps. Something like a board, certainly, firm under his arches. Very firm. Hard.

Then he knew.

He knew, and he could not move.

He was ice. But his knees melted, and he swung his arms to keep from falling.

He was on the very edge of his balcony, standing in the rim of the balcony wall, twelve stories up, and he swam in the air to save his life.

He struggled in the air, flailing, his body swaying back, and then leaning forward, pitching outward, the quaking aquamarine of the swimming pool shifting from one place to another as he fought.

He fell.

He twisted as he fell, and caught the wall of the balcony. His fingernails clawed concrete. The air was slammed from his body. But he fought hard, threw a leg over the wall and rocked there.

6

Don't look. He clenched his teeth. Do not look. He could not move, and he felt himself grow heavy. Heavier. Too heavy.

Whatever happens: don't look down.

He struggled back over the wall, and rolled onto the balcony floor. He shuddered, icy with sweat. He could not move. He thought only, I'm alive.

And then he realized a second, even more vivid truth: he had to change his life at once.

Or he would die.

PART One

1

Just before noon on Friday, the scaffolding snapped. The assembly of pipes and joints tumbled to the ground, and at first it was simply a mess. And then, in a heartbeat or two, the steel planks at the side fell in, the mud wall collapsed, and two men were buried.

Peter had been watching from the top of the trench. The English January had been mild, even here in York. The Northeast had not enjoyed such a mild winter in forty years, and the work on the dig had gone so well that Peter had loved every minute of it, even the mud and the rain.

And he had been enjoying the soft gray Yorkshire sky when the men were buried.

He slammed one hand over the top rung of the ladder, and plunged into the muck and water at the bottom, more than four meters down. He seized a mattock and hacked at the seethe of mud and stone.

Then he worked his arm in as far as it would go, his team around him, clawing mud. He dug with his bare hands. The mud was cold, and at first he was not sure he had gripped a shoe. His grip had slipped off at once, but he found it again, and this time he held on. His hand was going numb, but he squeezed as hard as he could. "I've got one!" he cried.

Strong hands joined him. A leg appeared, then two legs. An entire body spasmed and hunched out of the earth, and a big man, made even more huge with mud, sprawled at their feet.

Quick and precise work with a mattock, eager hands, and another man was dragged free. Earth seemed to hang on at the last moment, and the man, who looked like a featureless figure of muck, was inert, as though he had never been alive.

"Get a bucket of water down here," said Peter. He smoothed mud from first one face and then the other. Neither man spoke, and only the big man was even barely moving. Peter ran his hands over earth-coated clothing. He could not feel breath in either body. It was too late.

A black plastic bucket of water slopped down beside him. Jane knelt, a sponge in her hand, and tugged the helmet from the burly figure. The man grunted, a noise like a walrus coming up for air. A grin cracked the mask of mud. "I'm all right, Janey," croaked Skip's voice.

Peter emptied the bucket of water over the other man. Oliver, a much leaner man, still lay without a sound, and without so much as a tremor. Water flowed over his face, and his features began to appear. He was very pale beneath the mud. His rust red hair was clotted with earth. Peter put his hands on Oliver's neck, searching for a pulse. Jane fumbled for the buttons of the mud-clumsy shirt.

Peter pried open Oliver's mouth. He found the warm, quaking tongue with his finger, and made sure the throat passage was clear. Peter would be happy to save the life of any of his men. But Oliver, the cheerful and foul-mouthed Scot, was a man he especially liked. These were his two best men. It was brutal that these two, of all the men, should suffer this near disaster.

Peter had seen it coming. He had warned the office here in York, and he had warned London. But people never paid any attention to what Peter said. He had a reputation. Never mind Peter, people said. He goes on and on, always complaining, always in a foul temper. Nothing you can do for a man like Peter.

There had been a time, people said, when Peter had been not entirely right in the head.

Oliver coughed. He gagged, and tried to speak. Peter turned

Oliver's head, thinking that he needed to vomit. "What happened?" gasped Oliver.

"What happened," said Skip, climbing to his feet, a giant figure of earth, bearded and stout, "what happened was that the bank gave way, that's what happened."

Oliver crawled slowly to his feet, assisted by Jane. "I thought a building had fallen on me."

"Can you walk?" Peter asked both men.

"If you call this walking, I can walk," grunted Skip.

Dr. Hall at York District Hospital reported both men to be fine. "No evidence of anything but a minor concussion in the case of Mr. Stoughton. Quite lucky, actually."

"Lucky indeed," said Peter, grimly.

"What happened, exactly?" asked the doctor, a slim man with a spray of freckles across his face.

"Nobody believed me when I told them we had a problem."

Dr. Hall had no expression.

Nobody ever believes me, Peter nearly said. He said, "We had cheap scaffolding."

"Not the wisest way to save money," said the doctor.

Peter made the thinnest possible smile, and agreed.

Peter Chambers's Austin Minor sloshed through puddles up Wigginton Road, and he swerved to avoid a man on a bicycle on Gillygate. "Gate" was an old Norse word for street; many streets in York were called "Something-gate." Peter usually found this aspect of York charming, but nothing charmed him now.

Gravel spattered as he swung into the car park. He wrenched open the big wooden door and took the steps three at a time.

Mrs. Webster gazed at him over her tea and scone. She parted her lips, but did not have the opportunity to speak.

Peter slammed the door so violently that a page of the *Independent* on Langton's desk lifted and took a long moment to fall back. Langton looked up over his half-glasses. His plastic spoon was poised, laden with what looked like lemon yogurt.

"I heard about the trouble in Trench Five," said Langton.

"Did you."

"Good work on your part, from what I hear."

Peter could not stand still. He paced to the window. York Min-

13

ster was a slightly different shade of gray every time Peter saw it. Just now it was cigar-ash gray in the mist.

"I warned you about it," snapped Peter.

"We're proud to have a man on the spot like you, Peter."

This meant, Peter knew, that they had reservations about him, but that, for the moment, he was the best man they had.

"For some reason—the reason, I suppose, was money—the Foundation decided to rent equipment from the cheapest business in the North. Don't interrupt, please, Mr. Langton. Two of my men were nearly killed. To save a pound or two. Pipe bent up like pipe cleaners. I complain, and all I hear is reassurance of the most empty sort. 'Carry on, old son.' A wave of the hand. It's a wonder you give us helmets to wear."

The Northeast Archaeological Foundation was a recently privatized institute, overseen by a committee of distinguished scientists and bankers in London. Langton was one of the less distinguished administrators. This is why, Peter supposed, he was here in York, working with the actual men and women doing the grimy labor, and not in London gazing at ledger sheets.

"But," Langton was saying, "they were wearing their helmets?"

"Yes."

"I'm glad to hear that. We must have our people wearing their helmets. May have saved a life or two today, unless I'm terribly mistaken." Langton was not eating yogurt, after all. It was Sainsbury's Gooseberry Fool.

Peter strode to the desk and struck it with his fist. A spot of fool sprang from the spoon to a photograph of Princess Anne. Peter could not speak. It was impossible. The room flickered in his vision. He was beginning to feel the way he had felt during his bad years as a very young man, when his temper had been so terrible. Everyone remembered those bad times. They were on his record. They all wanted him to slip so they could find someone else to do his job.

Langton remembered. It was in his eyes, in his too careful smile. "You've done such good work, Peter. Really fine work."

Peter still could not speak.

"But it's all been a bit much, hasn't it? You've learned to master that temper of yours, and I admire that, actually. A man who can improve himself. Very admirable. But the pressure is getting to you, Peter, don't you think?"

It was really impossible. Peter was a professional, widely pub-

14

lished—a scientist. And here he was a puppet, manipulated by bureaucrats. Worse than that. Stupid bureaucrats.

"I was going to have a good long chat with you, sooner or later, so we may as well have it now." Langton seemed more than unruffled. He seemed cheered.

Peter fell into a chair. He could not bear to look at Langton.

"Good. A little chat," said Langton. "The finds department has been lagging a good bit, hasn't it?"

"I'm working twenty hours a day—"

"Exactly. That's it. Overworked, and all in a good cause, and we do appreciate it. You've been the best man for the job, Peter. The best."

Through his anger, Peter could sense that he should pay close attention to what Langton was about to say. He clasped his hands together.

"I've just had a word with Dr. Higg," Langton continued. "Or, rather, he's had a word with me. He rang me from London. He was especially concerned when he heard of this business with the mud."

Peter closed his eyes. The near disaster which had nearly killed two men would be forever trivialized in Langton's mind as "this business with the mud." And, eventually, "that muddy business we had at one point." Higg, though, was an important man, and Peter had respect for him. He was a former barrister turned archaeologist, an adviser to several governments. His list of honors was a long train of abbreviations after his name, and just three months before he had been made a papal knight. Higg was the sole bureaucrat who had any knowledge of what it was like to wield a mattock.

"He was so concerned, and so proud of you, Peter. So very proud. 'That Chambers is a quick thinker,' is what he said when I told him what had happened. And I certainly second that. But he said, and I quite agree, that it's about time you had some help here in York. With the finds, with the paperwork, all the nasty bits, while you get on with the business in the field."

Peter was expected to make some sort of response. He grunted, and looked away. He had to admit that he liked working with his hands. He enjoyed getting dirty in the name of archaeology, and did not especially like entering finds numbers into a computer, although he knew this was essential.

"We don't want this sort of thing to recur. Not that we blame you—"

"Me!"

"Not a bit. But to make the entire effort go more smoothly. London does provide the money, you know. York is a mere appendage, and we must bow to their wiser counsel."

"Naturally," said Peter, with some bitterness. He had calmed himself, however. Just stay quiet, he told himself. Don't talk, and you won't say anything you regret.

"And I think you'll like Dr. Higg's suggestion. He has put forward the name of a man I believe you know, a really gifted scientist, and an expert at finds. Quite an author, as well, of the more technical sort of book. An old colleague—Davis Lowry."

Langton smiled expectantly.

Peter stood and paced. Davis was the last person in the world he could work with. He could not even stand to be in the same room with Davis.

Peter fell back into his chair and met Langton's gaze. Peter could not forgive Langton for this. Actually, it was Higg's responsibility. Langton was droning, smiling, nodding. "You'll make an outstanding team, really, I'm sure you'll agree."

Archaeology was an international affair. Peter had been born in Leeds, but he had studied in London and Mexico City and had taught for three years in Los Angeles. He had worked, however briefly, on every continent. Word of marriages and divorces, successes and failures, traveled the globe, but the bureaucrats, even perceptive men like Higg in London, did not hear all the gossip. The bureaucrats had, in perfect ignorance, made the worst possible choice.

"I'm delighted," said Peter with such sarcasm that anyone but a cretin like Langton would have gotten up and locked the door.

But Peter consoled himself. Davis was not a complete idiot. He was, in truth, quite bright. And he was a gifted specialist when it came to finds. Peter would be able to stay in the field with Jane. It was Jane that mattered now. Margaret was a part of the past. Jane was the future.

Peter did something that was, for him, rare. He decided to give someone a fresh start. Maybe it would be good to work with Davis. At least Davis was not a bureaucrat. Peter took a long, deep breath and let it go.

Peter stood and thrust forth his hand. "There's work to be done."

"Always, always," beamed Langton. "We're in such a busy business."

Peter reassured himself again: at least Davis would not be like Langton.

Peter stopped by York District Hospital and sat beside Oliver's bed. The man had seemed asleep, but he opened his eyes. "They're making me fucking stay overnight," he said.

"It's hardly a surprise, is it? You were buried alive today."

"All in a day's work, Peter," said Oliver cheerfully. "It's not the last strange thing we'll see."

Peter smiled, but he did not understand.

"Look at you, like you haven't heard. Everyone talks about it."

"About what?"

"Everybody knows. You mean you haven't heard?"

"Enlighten me."

"You'll see some interesting things happen down on Skeldergate where we're digging."

Peter inclined his head to say, Tell me more.

"And you don't know why?" Oliver's eyes were bright.

"I haven't a clue."

"Because the site has a ghost."

Peter laughed.

Oliver smiled cheerfully, but with a trace of cunning. "I didn't fucking believe in it, either, Peter. But I do now. Skip and I checked that scaffolding this morning, Peter. There was nothing wrong with it."

Peter found himself smiling uncomfortably.

"There's nothing you can do about it, Peter. The place is haunted."

Peter tortured the Austin's engine, driving the medieval streets at criminal speed, and squealed to a stop at the dig. The dozen or so workers were attending to their various tasks, and three men had begun the apparently hopeless task of clearing the mud from Trench Five, with Jane overseeing them.

One of the men was Alf, the most tattooed man on the site.

Peter called to him, and Alf scrambled out of the trench and into the main Portakabin.

Alf had snakes on his arms, and a dragon peeking from under his shirt collar. He sat, caked with mud as he was, in a chair that had long ago ceased to be clean. His black hair was an arrangement of messy spikes. He offered Peter some cigarette tobacco from a tin of Golden Virginia, and Peter accepted with thanks.

"Tell me about the ghost," said Peter, smoking.

"What is this all about then, Peter? You call me in to talk about a ghost? Who told you to do that? Oliver?"

"You know all the important things, Alf. Are the men talking about a ghost?"

"Men talk, don't they? That's a natural thing, isn't it?" A Yorkshire smile, and that warmth Peter missed whenever he traveled. "But you know, Peter, there is a haunting or—or a Something about, isn't there. All these little things that have been happening. And now the bad accident in Trench Five. I don't worry myself, like, but some of the men might."

"A ghost."

"Nobody actually believes in such things, do they? But think of all the peculiar little things that have happened. The tools that have gone missing, and the way the coffee cups have moved about every night."

But Peter could not consider a ghost. He could think only of Davis Lowry.

They had both loved the same woman, Margaret Rawlings, a brilliant archaeologist with a limitless future. She could have worked in Olduvai with Peter. She could have hiked the Andes with Peter. She could have done that long-overdue survey of Kos with Peter, who wanted her, and needed her. Instead she had married Davis, and had become a housewife in California, a helper, not a companion. He had heard the gossip from fellow archaeologists. Everyone else was sympathetic to Davis. Peter knew what had happened. No one had to tell him. Because she had married such an egocentric man she had begun to drink, and then her life had crumbled until she had died in such an agonizing and spectacular way that Peter could not stand to think about it.

"Oliver told you to ask me, didn't he?" Alf said, smiling. "That man's a scamp, he is. It takes more than a wall of rock falling on him to teach him any sense. Oliver thinks I'm superstitious."

"Are you?"

"I believe in what happens, Peter. And what happens here is very strange."

"Little accidents happen on every dig. I don't want you encouraging the other men to believe in—whatever you believe."

Alf laughed. "There's a ghost, Peter. But I won't talk about him."

2

The Foundation was excavating near the river Ouse, on Skeldergate. Several late nineteenth-century buildings had been demolished, and the law allowed archaeologists to study the site before a new building was erected. The preliminary examination had exposed wonders. They had uncovered the rugged remains of an Anglo-Saxon tower, evidently a riverside stronghold. Digging deeper in another trench—they weren't trenches so much as large rectangular chasms—a Roman road surface was scraped bare. They were in the midst of the richest finds most of them had ever seen.

They had found Norse antler-pin jewelry and peat-blackened sandals. There were middens and filled-in wells, and, on one later afternoon, a black and slimy leather sack was brushed free of the last damp earth, disclosing, through a split in the leather, the glint of red fire. It was a hoard of gold sceatas, hidden for over a thousand years.

But now the site had a new look in Peter's eyes. It was the day after the cave-in, and Peter had found it hard to sleep the night before. All this talk of ghosts was disturbing. No, not disturbing—not at all. It was irritating. There had been little accidents since the very start of excavation here. Unimportant little events. A broken window, a fire in a rubbish bin, missing folders. Tools that had been hung up tidily in the tool cabin had been jumbled and heaped on the floor by morning.

He could not sit still at his desk, so he found some manual labor to do. There was always plenty of that.

People were going to say that Peter Chambers was still a bit strange, after all these years. The Skeldergate dig had been plagued by very unusual accidents, and the men talked of nothing but ghosts. Tell me this, they would say. Would that happen with a normal site supervisor?

The generator, a noisy machine on wheels like a small tractor, rumbled. The pneumatic drill clattered, powered by the lavender Silensair air compressor. Every hand was busy. Peter emptied the buckets of earth as they were winched from Trench Five. Jane was shoveling, and Mandy was hefting buckets and hooking them onto the winch rope.

Jane was lithe, with delicate features, but she could shovel as well as any man. Mandy was a dumpling, blue-eyed and red-cheeked, and she handled a mattock—a pick with a broad, flat blade—easily. The science of archaeology had highly trained women working beside men—like Oliver and Skip—who were hired laborers. Everyone involved worked with enthusiasm, and with care.

The wheelbarrow was full, and Peter wheeled it along the plank track and emptied it. He wheeled the empty barrow back and emptied another bucketful into it. Jane and Mandy were clearing the trench of the mud that had nearly taken two lives. It was unscreened earth, and so the work had to go slowly. There might be an artifact hidden in the muck. It was late afternoon, and although it was January, it was only chilly, not actually cold.

Peter hated to be a nuisance. They were working so steadily. But he finally climbed down into the trench himself, and began filling buckets. "I'm beginning to be worried that we won't have it all dug out by dark."

Jane straightened and gazed at him, tucking a wisp of hair under her yellow helmet. "We're working quickly, Peter, actually," she said, with enough courtesy to disclose her irritation.

"Right," said Peter. "I know you are. I can bring some men out of Trench Nine."

"I think we can cope," smiled Jane. Peter knew that as far as she was concerned, the wage-earning shovel and mattock men were sturdy but inept. This was sensitive work, and required professional hands.

Peter stooped, and flicked a splinter of bone into the black plastic finds tray. It might be the remains of a Norseman's dinner, or a fragment of Anglo-Saxon jewelry.

"I think we can finish by dark fairly easily, Peter," Jane was saying. But Jane was one of the reasons Peter hovered here. Jane: the future. Simply seeing her work with a trowel, or tuck a loose lock of hair into her helmet, was enough to make Peter feel his entire life change.

"You were more help up top emptying buckets," said Mandy. She had that bright milkmaid's smile, and dimpled elbows.

"Perhaps this is one of those afternoons when you should go play with your toys, Peter," said Jane, in a kind tone. "Really. We can manage this quite well."

This reference to his "toys" made Peter wince, and he smiled to disguise his annoyance. For years he had loved cars and airplanes that could be operated by remote control. He had designed cars himself, and had patented several improvements for remote-controlled Cessnas. Sundays tended to find him in a field north of York, commanding one of his remote-controlled airplanes. They were scarcely toys. They were examples of a science of the sort Leonardo would have relished.

Strangely, he had supposed that Jane admired his knowledge. He had taken her flying with him just a few weeks ago. It had been a special afternoon. Now it seemed she took this science lightly. Still, he smiled. He was standing in ground water that was very cold, and the color of Rowntree's cocoa. He was a hard man to discourage.

He picked up a shovel from the muck, took a scoop of the sloppy mud, and hit his head on the scaffolding.

Hard. He was not wearing his helmet. Langton would not have been surprised. Peter bent double, tears in his eyes, a taste in his mouth like warm salt water. He touched a knuckle to his lips. He had bitten them.

Jane slipped a helmet over his head, and made soothing sounds. "It's a terrible thing, Peter. Are you all right?"

"I'm in the way," said Peter at last. "Carry on. Go on, both of you. Keep working."

He eyed the supports. They looked strong. They had looked

strong yesterday. Perhaps the cheapness of the steel pipes had nothing to do with their collapse.

It was dangerous here. "Maybe we've done enough for one day," he said.

"We'll be very careful," said Jane.

He could not bear it if anything happened to her.

But he was being foolish. Accidents could be prevented. There were no unseen powers here. He touched her hand. "Please be careful."

"Go on up and man the wheelbarrow," she said.

He had one foot on the ladder. The thin steel rungs did not look strong enough to support his muddy boot. Careful, he told himself. Be very careful. He began to pull himself up the ladder, when Jane's voice stopped him.

"Peter!" she called again.

He had never heard this thrill in her voice before. He dropped from the ladder, and splashed through the mud.

"Peter, there's something here."

There was more in her voice than a simple thrill. It was something more. Something like horror.

"I can't see anything," said Peter.

"Here." As she extended her hand, her forefinger stretched to touch another finger extended, blackly, from the earth.

His first thought was, Someone is buried here. It's one of my men!

But this was not one of his men. It couldn't be. The finger was ebony and glistening, and as Peter knelt to examine it he began to understand what he was seeing.

Nearly all of the mud which had collapsed into the trench had been cleared. The falling mud had exposed a new surface in the trench wall. The surface here was peat-consistency, with decayed wood and leaves and scraps of timber, some of it charred. The collapse of the wall had exposed this pit of long-ago rotted vegetation.

This blackened finger silenced them.

"I need my trowel," said Jane softly.

Mandy slipped Jane's trowel into her hand. Archaeologists have favorite trowels, tools worn in just the right places. Jane dug deftly, chipping the decayed vegetation from around the finger. Mandy used a white tape to measure the finger, and quickly sketched the find surface on grid paper. She fumbled for the Minolta, and took a series of snaps while Jane worked.

Jane gently flicked away specks of carbonized plant. Her trowel made a faint chiming sound. As she worked, it was as though the hand reached out toward her, because that is exactly what it was. A perfect hand.

Mandy's pencil scratched. She turned a page and began another sketch.

Jane met Peter's eyes. They had found human bones before, even the skull of an infant in Trench One. But this was not a skeleton. This was a hand, complete with fingernails. Examined closely, the mud brushed away, the swirls of the fingerprints were clear.

Peter hesitated. He lifted his hand. He paused.

He touched it.

Immediately, he shrank back. The hand was cold, earth-cold, groundwater-cold. And it was something else, something that made his pulse hammer.

It was supple. It had moved as the weight of his touch pressed upon it, as flexible as the hand of a man just dead. Or a man who was merely asleep. The fingers were relaxed, the palm upturned, like someone who was dreaming.

Peter whispered, "I'll ring Dr. Higg. We mustn't tell anyone else until we find out what he wants us to do."

The hand gleamed in the late afternoon.

"We'll get the high-powered torches out of storage," he added. "We can work all night."

The groundwater splashed, and the electric light glittered. They stretched canvas across the trench. They continued to work into the night, long after everyone else had left the site.

As they worked, the arm extended itself toward them, farther and farther, reaching. The skin of the arm had a sheen, like the most expensive leather. There were fine hairs on the arm, blond against the dark skin. The arm moved, just slightly, when Peter brushed it, or when Jane worked under it with the trowel.

They were afraid to speak. More and more of the arm reached out toward them from the black earth. At last, Peter motioned for them to stop. The time had come for them to discover what it was they had before them. Was it only a limb, or was it an entire, preserved human being?

3

Davis fell across the bed. He did not expect to sleep. Birds were squabbling outside, and bright sun leaked through the curtains. He could never sleep after a long flight, and he still did not trust himself to sleep. Even here in England, where, he knew, all would be well.

His mind was a jumble. The packed 747. Dr. Higg's wonderful smile greeting him at Heathrow. The terrible traffic, until at last they passed the Maida Vale station and turned the corner to Dr. Higg's house in St. John's Wood. It was wonderful to be here. In a few minutes he would rouse himself and walk up to Abbey Road.

He slept.

When he woke it was dark. He bathed and shaved. He felt like a man reprieved from death. He felt remarkably well, in fact.

Dr. Higg waved Davis into a chair. "Scottish trout and Montrachet," he said, "after we do a bit of work."

"I'm looking forward to work," said Davis. "I need it."

"We have plenty of that. And we need you, Davis. Rather badly, I'm afraid."

Dr. Higg had a large face, with creases that made him resemble a hound. Firelight glittered in his eyes, however, and they were not the eyes of a sleepy, comfortable animal. Higg studied Davis, as though looking into Davis's soul.

Davis imagined that his soul, if it could be observed, was a mess. He had called Dr. Higg as soon as he realized that he had to change his life immediately. "I need a project," he had said. "Something that involves a lot of work. And I need it now. I can't wait."

Davis accepted a drink, one of those smoke-rich whiskeys Higg had always favored. Higg had been Davis's teacher at York University some fifteen years before. Davis thought he knew Higg well, and yet the man's evident intelligence always surprised him.

"You had no trouble getting medical leave?" asked Higg.

"They understood completely."

"I have one or two treasures," said Dr. Higg. His voice was alive with pleasure. "There is this lovely golden circlet, Anglo-Saxon, although not from York. It looks, I think, like a moon in eclipse. It was found near Ely. Some say it belonged to one of the kings—perhaps the King of the Fenmen."

It was a delicate, perfect circle, the blood-and-sunlight glow of ancient gold. Higg set it aside. "I will show you the other treasure, from our current dig, in a moment. But first I must tell you what is happening in York. And I really don't know how to begin."

Dr. Higg glanced away for a moment. "There are troubles, Davis. Mysterious troubles."

Davis knew enough to wait, and listen. Dr. Higg leaned back in his leather chair. "The dig on York has become even more important than I thought when we first talked." Dr. Higg sighed. "I thought, when you called, that this work would be the best thing for you."

"I was losing my mind." Davis explained again, as he had over the telephone. His waking dreams. His sleepwalking. How badly he missed Margaret, and how much he needed to work.

Dr. Higg smiled sadly. "And, of course, work is the cure for sorrow. I understand you well, Davis. Or I think I do. You want to join Margaret. You want to die, and be with her."

Davis shrank back into the leather. The truth had a sharpness to it, a chill. He watched the fire. A part of him, it was no doubt true, did want to join Margaret in death. But a stronger part of him wanted to live. Dr. Higg, however, did not know the entire truth.

Dr. Higg turned, and placed a wooden box on his knee. "We need you among the living, Davis."

The evident kindness and sincerity behind this statement brought tears to Davis's eyes.

"And we particularly need your help in York. There have been serious troubles, and we need your experienced hand."

Dr. Higg described the unexplained accidents that had troubled the Skeldergate site since the beginning, and shook his head as he described the collapse of the bank in Trench Five. "Peter Chambers worked quickly. You know the man. Can be very firm, and very much the right man when you need a hole dug, or a man pulled out of an avalanche. But it is precisely Peter who has me most troubled."

"I worked with him—"

"At York, back when we were all together. I remember, and quite well. But there are things that his colleagues generally don't know about Peter. He has had a troubled past. I suppose I can speak in confidence, and fairly explicitly. He had psychiatric problems as a very young man. You are all in your late thirties, and I had hoped Peter had gotten his emotional legs under him by now. And I always admired his energy. A good man, in many ways. So we took a risk. It was my responsibility."

"I hadn't realized that Peter had such troubles. A temper, as I recall."

"He had very serious troubles." Dr. Higg opened the box on his lap and took out a rust-crippled object.

"What sort of troubles—" Davis began, but then he decided that he really didn't want to know. He remembered Peter Chambers as a competent, serious scientist.

Dr. Higg held the red-black object in the light from the fireplace. His expression softened as he gazed at it. "This is one of the finds I asked them to send down to me from York. You know what it is."

Davis did not hesitate. "Norse sword hilt, Danish iron, dating from eight hundred, give or take twenty years on either side. If we could read it, it would have a prayer on the crosspiece in Roman letters. It's a larger than usual example."

"Ceremonial, I should imagine. Lovely." Dr. Higg returned it to its box. "You ask what sort of problems Peter suffered, and I hesitate to even talk about them. I'll be brief. You might as well know the truth about Peter. He tortured animals to death."

27

"Good Lord."

"Throughout his career, and I've been watching him from a distance for years, he has continued to outgrow his early problems. But lately, I have become concerned. This site has developed into a very strange place. Peculiar things tend to happen there. Just the odd accident, you understand. But Peter's calls to me have begun to sound strained. He has difficulties with Langton, his immediate superior. I have begun to be concerned. Perhaps this assignment is too much for him."

He set the box aside. "And now there's this. This newest discovery. It will be world famous. Equal to the Bog Men of Denmark." He tugged a folder from the table beside him. "Really something most unusual."

Davis was accustomed to airy understatement from Dr. Higg. There was the slightest trembling in his hand as he reached for the folder. And the slightest hesitation. Then he took the folder and put it on his lap. He did not open it.

"Go ahead and open it. You won't be disappointed."

The folder fell open.

He studied the black-and-white glossies. The photographs nearly slipped from his fingers. There had been several bog men over the years, bodies discovered preserved in peat tannin. Most had suffered some degree of decay or deformation.

This body was perfect.

Davis could not speak.

"Quite," said Dr. Higg. "I feel exactly as you do."

Davis closed the folder. "How are they keeping it?"

"We are relying on the experience of past bog finds. Some people say keep them wet. Some say keep them dry. We are keeping our man dry, in a stable environment. Quite literally under lock and key. What happens to him next is entirely under your jurisdiction."

"When is the last train out of King's Cross?"

"You certainly don't have to leap out of your chair like that. I was just beginning to feel cozy myself, and just about to consider another whiskey."

Davis waved the folder. "This is the opportunity of a lifetime!"

"Yes, I quite agree. But you'll arrive in York at well after midnight, dear Davis. I can't imagine how you'll get into your flat. I can ring Peter, I suppose, but he can be a bit nasty on the telephone."

* * *

Davis caught the ten o'clock from King's Cross, and the distant lights of houses and cars drifted slowly past in the darkness. Davis knew that by daylight the countryside would have been serene and winter green.

Now he had his own reflection for company, and a single drunken young man, whose nose was bleeding. Two other young men in black leather lurched down the train and sat on the arms of chairs. They showed off how they could fight nonexistent opponents, punching the air and laughing.

Everyone but Davis got off at Peterborough, and he had, it seemed, the entire train to himself. The black country stared back, and one or two lights floated by.

Ahead of him, across the night, a twelve-hundred-year-old man was waiting.

4

The station was empty. The gates had been shut, except for one at the far end through which Davis huddled. It was colder here in the Northeast. It had been years since he had seen the city walls of York, and he strained to see a familiar landmark. The walls were dark. His luggage clattered behind him on its wheels. A sole figure worked past on a bicycle, barely illuminated by a streetlight. The cold wind made Davis take a step backward for a moment. He gathered his coat about him, and peered into the cold for some sign of Peter.

But there was no one. Not even a taxi. He had no idea where to go.

A hand gripped his arm.

"I didn't forget you," said Peter.

Bundled into a very small, pale Austin, Davis shivered in the gust of apparently freezing air from the car heater. "Your flat is just above mine," said Peter.

"Take me to the find."

"There'll be time for that in the morning."

"Take me to it now. Please."

"Good," said Peter. "I was hoping you would say that."

Peter stood on the brakes, and they waited at a stoplight, unnecessarily, it seemed to Davis. There were no other cars. "It's more amazing than you think," said Peter. "The photographs can't begin to show how astounding it is."

"Where are you—we—keeping it?"

Peter slammed the car into first, and the tires squealed. The light was still red. "We have a lab in the cellar of Saint Andrews College. It's a very secure place, and the facilities are good."

"Any sign of post-find deterioration?"

"None. We have it sealed, of course. And its future depends a good deal on what you decide to do. But perhaps I shouldn't refer to our friend as 'it.' 'He' is entirely more appropriate."

"What else do we know—aside from his sex?"

"You sound cold."

"I'm excited. And cold, too."

"You'll be even more excited when you see him."

"You sound like you're hiding something."

"I'm just keeping an odd little secret about our new friend. You'll see what it is."

They had all worked together at a dig beside the Ouse, east of York. Margaret and Peter and Davis had not been close, but they had enjoyed each other's company. And perhaps Margaret had been fond of Peter. Davis couldn't remember. Perhaps there had been something between them.

Since then, Davis had gone on to several other digs in Britain, including the dig that had uncovered the theater in Saint Albans. The dig at Tulum, in the Yucatán, had established Davis's career. His book on that dig, *Mayan Blood, Mayan Gold,* which he had begun as a day-by-day journal, had become popular enough to establish him as a photogenic, scholarly scientist, expert enough to be taken seriously in the profession, and good-looking and articulate enough to warrant tours of television talk shows.

Peter had the same sharp profile Davis remembered. Perhaps a little more sharp than it had been. He drove with the same edge-of-fury eagerness that Davis recalled. Peter had published in many of the professional quarterlies, and had specialized in Davis's own first love, Anglo-Saxon artifacts. But Peter had not enjoyed—or been distracted by—the kind of popular success which had fallen to Davis. Peter was a scientist's scientist, and Davis admired this. Davis was, at times, slightly embarrassed at his public image. He preferred the Peter Chambers sort of archaeologist, a man who went about the business of discovering the past. It would be good to work with Peter again.

The car fishtailed and lurched to a stop. Peter leaped from the car, and Davis followed. Great skeletal trees reached above him into the wind. As he watched, a star was blotted by black.

St. Andrews College was a handsome series of brick buildings and a nineteenth-century Gothic chapel, surrounded by black trees. In the dark, Davis had to use his imagination to see the green lawns and the age-charred red brick. The city walls of York were behind the two men as they hurried through the cold. A key tinkled, and they descended stairs. A naked bulb cast bad light. A steel door required two keys, and there was yet another, colder, darker set of stairs.

"They did top-secret work here during the war," said Peter. "Developed superior sulfa drugs, and they were afraid the German spies might get a hold of the secret." His breath was white in the half light, each syllable a plume. "Since then, scientists have used it for their most sensitive work. They had typhoid bacillus here at one time, trying to develop antidotes to it in case of germ warfare during the fifties."

Davis reflected that despite his troubled past, Peter sounded entirely competent, completely lucid. Perhaps Dr. Higg's fears were completely unfounded.

The third door, an even thicker slab of steel, did not open. Peter worked the key, grunting with the effort. "Dr. Higg arranged for us to have this lab as soon as he heard about our find."

"When did you discover him?"

"Just a fortnight ago."

A few days, thought Davis, after I walked off my twelfth-story balcony.

"We needed the lab space, anyway," Peter was saying. "Virtually no one knows this lab is here. I suppose it doesn't matter to us, but it's considered bombproof."

Fluorescent lights stuttered, and went out. And then blinked, and stayed on.

There were banks of lab tables, of the sort suitable for dissection of human cadavers. There were stainless steel sinks, and cupboards. Finds trays were stacked along one wall. A peek into one showed paper tags and scraps of pottery and bone. A sample of the work ahead of him, Davis considered cheerfully. Doors opened to offices. And at the far end of the vast room locked doors sealed off, he guessed, yet more lab space.

It was cold. It smelled of earth and damp. They were underground. Davis paused. He did not want to step any closer to those sealed doors.

Run away. Don't go any closer. Don't let him open the door. Because he knew which door it was. It was that door. That one there. This was the moment his career had waited for, and yet all he could think was, Don't open that door.

He was a fool. He could not begin to understand his strange reluctance.

"You're still shivering," said Peter, not unkindly. "I can't say I blame you. It's always freezing down here. We have a few portable heaters set about, enough to warm our toes."

Don't open that door.

Another key found a lock, and a bolt clicked. The door opened, silently. There was only more darkness. Peter put his hand into the dark, as though afraid to enter it.

"It's the perfect place to keep him," said Davis.

He shrank back, away from the sudden light in the room just before him.

Peter beckoned him forward.

The doorway was a rectangle of light. This room was even colder. The walls were the off-green favored by governments around the world. It was the green of a post office in Dallas, and the airport in Izmir.

This was the green tiled floor of a hospital. Or a morgue. There was a single dissection table, waist high. On the table was a plastic blanket, thick and black. Under the plastic was the unmistakable shape of a human figure. Davis breathed into his hands.

Perhaps Dr. Higg was right. Perhaps he wanted to join Margaret.

He was being foolish. Now that he was in England, all his troubled times were behind him. Impatient with himself, he gripped a corner of the black plastic, and flung it back.

A smaller black plastic bag glistened under the light. A body bag, Davis found himself thinking. His hand crept toward the zipper, found the tab, and began to tug the zipper down, the tiny teeth releasing with a loud rasp in the great stillness of the room.

When the bag was unzipped all the way, Davis seized the upper half of the plastic and whisked it aside, and then stepped back, until the wall pushed him from behind.

He had not been prepared for this.

Before him was a perfect, sleeping man. He was as dark as the darkest coffee. He was unshaven—there was the white gloss of two or three days' beard on his chin and cheeks. He wore a tunic of coarse wool, tar black, and reduced to rags. One hand stretched forth, as though it had just stopped moving. The head was slightly turned to one side.

A dreamer.

In a moment of blank horror, Davis saw his own hand stretch forth, hesitate, and close around the wrist. To his disbelief, he found himself seeking a pulse.

There was no pulse. His hand closed around the wrist as it would close around an empty boot leg. The arm was boneless. Davis shrank back, squeezing his own wrist. He had expected this, of course. The tannic acid that had preserved this body had dissolved most of the bones. And yet, it had surprised him.

Davis saw the secret Peter had referred to. It was easy to miss it, at first. He looked up, and Peter nodded.

"That's it," said Peter.

There was a second mouth in the man's throat, a gaping slit. His throat had been cut.

"He was murdered," Davis whispered.

"It does look that way."

"I'll do a complete examination," said Davis, perhaps too briskly, "as soon as I can."

"There's an excellent assistant I might suggest. A young woman from New Delhi called Irene Saarni. She's very experienced at handling such finds."

"I could use her help," said Davis, thankful to be discussing procedure. It took his mind off the ancient wound before him under the bitter light.

Then Davis stirred himself. His dazed expression must look anything but professional. "Yes, please ask her to see me. We'll do a postmortem—a considerably-post mortem I guess I'd have to call it. How did you transport him?"

"We covered him with polystyrene pellets. The body turns out,

34

actually, to be quite supple, but we assumed it was fragile, and treated it as though it were made of glass."

"I imagine the CAT scan will show fairly good preservation of intercranial contents. That's usual in such cases. Teeth are visible, without manipulating the mandible." Davis fished the tape recorder out of his inner jacket pocket. He thumbed the button. The teeth were black, as though carved out of charcoal. "Both the color of the teeth and the spacing indicate loss of enamel. The teeth are really quite far apart. We can measure later."

He wiggled his fingers to show what he needed, and Peter opened a drawer. Davis tugged on a pair of surgical gloves. He bent closer to examine the wound on the throat.

"We didn't rule out the possibility that the apparent wound was postmortem, due to tissue stress," Peter was saying.

"I'm afraid not. I'm afraid he was murdered. The superior border of the right lamina of the thyroid cartilage has been cut. This is a wound entirely consistent with a blade of some sort. An especially sharp blade."

"He bled to death."

"I'm afraid so. I wish— it sounds pointless, but I wish he had suffered a heart attack. There's something about this I don't like."

Peter seemed reluctant to speak for a moment. "Some of the hired men refused to come anywhere near the trench. They joked about it. But they said—well, they didn't like the fact that he'd been found at all, and when rumor got about that he'd been murdered. . . . You might be surprised how much superstition there is about."

"Maybe there was a fight. We'll look for fractures, but with so much calcium gone—"

"He weighs about thirty pounds."

The pubic hair was ginger, and the penis and scrotum well preserved, although slightly atrophied. Fingernails and toenails were all present. "An examination under magnification will be interesting. We'll want to know if he was a laborer. His unshaven appearance makes him look like someone who was normally clean-shaven but who for some reason neglected his toilet in the last days of his life."

"I get the impression," said Peter, "that he was usually fairly tidy. The nails are close-cropped. His hair is as short as mine."

"I wonder why he hadn't shaved."

"Perhaps he was in hiding."

"If so, they certainly found him. Not much callus on his feet or hands. His clothes are pretty gunked-up with peat. No jewelry. Anything on the site yet?"

"We're going very slowly. No jewelry yet."

"And no murder weapon?"

The truth seemed to close around the two men. They had a murder victim who had been dead for over a thousand years, and they were talking as though they were detectives considering a fresh crime. Time seemed to have stopped mattering. This man had lost his life. Davis wanted justice for him. And he felt compassion for this victim. And for his friends, and his family, all vanished, centuries ago.

"Were the police notified?"

"Naturally. But as soon as they saw it they knew it wasn't a case for them. The C-fourteen tests came back from three different labs just yesterday. Plus or minus three hundred years, he's twelve hundred years old."

It was still dark, but it was a predawn dark. The Minster, that great cathedral, pierced the black like a stone giant made beautiful by a spell. The stones of Bootham Bar, turreted, ancient, seemed to glow from within.

Peter drove fast, the tires squealing as he spun into Saint Mary's. He shifted gears, punishing the tiny car, and hissed to a stop beside a row of rubbish bins.

The two men banged up the stairs with Davis's luggage, climbing in virtual darkness. "We have a name for him," said Peter. "Several names, actually. Every bog man has a name. We had a few names which we rejected. Minster Man. That's a stupid name. York Man is an adequate name, but hardly a name to stir the breast. Here, stop by my flat for a drink. You can climb all the way to the top later. Private Funds Man would please the bureaucrats."

They sat in the cramped kitchen. Peter poured gin into two glasses. "So my thought is to name him after the road on which the dig is located. Skeldergate. What do you think?"

Davis lifted his glass. "Here's to our friend. The Skeldergate Man."

Peter shook out a pouch of Samson. He sprinkled tobacco into a sheet of Rizla, and watched Davis from the corner of his eye. Davis had always had that square jaw. He was blond, and looked as intelligent as he was. But he was, as well, a man who had been through hell. The look in his eyes was not simple travel fatigue. Peter guessed that losing Margaret had been a terrible thing for Davis. That, and the fact that his observations regarding the Skeldergate Man had all been remarkably professional, convinced Peter that Davis would, indeed, not be so difficult to work with. Besides, perhaps Peter owed it to his memory of Margaret.

"I was terribly sorry to hear about Margaret," said Peter. "We were all so awfully fond of her."

The sound of her name turned Davis away, like a man struck across the face. Davis thanked him, and said that he had nearly lost his mind.

Peter rattled the red box of Winner's matches, and lit his cigarette. "Another drink?"

In a voice without self-pity, Davis told him about his sleep-walking, and about the nightmares he had suffered. "The hard part is that I am always, at first, very happy to see her."

Peter listened, and did not show his surprise that such a solid-looking man could be so close to losing his sanity. Even now, he was not quite sound of mind. Davis would still need a great deal of time. He was still not a man ready for all the confusion and pain the world could give him.

"You want cheering up, is what you want," said Peter. "Come into the sitting room for a moment."

It was too large to be a toy, but that's apparently what it was. It was red and white, and it was heavy. It was not the flimsy, tiny plastic car Davis had known as a boy.

"It's a Grabber four-wheel drive. You operate it with one of these little black boxes. Taiyo two-channel radio controls. It's a hobby—or a passion—of mine. That, and radio-controlled flight. I suppose there are some things one never actually outgrows."

Davis found himself holding a black box with a single telescoping antenna. He switched one dial, and then another. The machine at his side growled. He set it on the carpet, and it flipped over against the leg of a chair. "I need a little practice."

"You can't hurt it. It's got a polycarbonate body—fairly strong."

Davis set the car on its wheels again, and it sped toward the wall. It collided with the metal grid of the artificial fireplace, a heater with plastic coals. The heater resounded with the force of the crash.

The car would not respond.

"Here," said Peter. "A battery fell out. It uses eight one-point-five batteries, these red ones. Called double A in the U.S."

"You must go through a lot of batteries."

"I have a recharger—only cost seven pounds fifty. I take a Cessna or a Spitfire flying up the river, when the weather allows. I've always loved R-C devices. I just wanted you to know it won't be all bog men and bones here in York."

The racing car snaked through the legs of the chair, and bounded over a wrinkle in the carpet. It vanished into the hall, and the whirring wheels continued, grinding faintly in the next room.

Peter twisted a dial with a boyish smile, lost, for a moment, in pleasure. The car threaded its way through unseen rooms.

"You have to have a good mental picture of where things are in the next room," said Peter. "This is more satisfying, in a way, than the airplanes, which you can see up there in the sky every moment. This is a challenge—missing bed legs and the odd discarded shoe. I must have run over a sock just now. It slowed down for a moment. Here it comes."

And then it was not fun.

The car was a wasplike drill somewhere in the next room, unseen, but guided by intelligence, nearly intelligent itself. It thudded over the hall carpet, and burst upon them.

It sought Davis. He lifted his feet, cringing involuntarily from the red-and-white demon. The devilish toy leaped, and spun through the air, and landed wheels upward in his lap. It was a sight Davis found surprisingly repulsive, like the many working legs of a trapped cockroach.

It struggled in his hands, and then went dead. He held it like a brilliant husk, the carapace of an amazing, bright-hued insect.

Peter had a look of glee on his face. It was not a pretty expression.

"I like tennis," said Davis, attempting to carry the conversation. "But I guess my favorite hobby would have to be snorkling."

"A difficult hobby to pursue here. Both the Foss and the Ouse are cold and fairly muddy. Mallards and moorhens, and visibility of about ten centimeters."

That momentary expression was gone. Peter looked sane again.

Davis described the parrot fish of Cozumel, and how hypnotic it had been to see a surge of silvery fish part around him. "They have an ugly name, those silver fish," said Davis. "French grunt."

"Let me show you to your flat."

His flat was smaller than Peter's. It had a view, from the bedroom window, of the Minster. The stone of the Minster, soaring, seemingly withered with its articulations and pinnacles, was pink with dawn.

Watch over me, he found himself thinking. He opened the window, and propped it with its notched slide. The roof was slate, sloping downward, and it was too cold to leave the window open for long.

The Minster did not, for the moment, seem so much a guardian as a threat.

5

"I will be able to help you," said the dark woman with curly black hair. "You need an assistant, don't you?"

"Very much," Davis agreed.

The woman lifted herself onto her toes for a moment, as though his answer amused her. "And so now you have one."

"Tell me a little about yourself."

"I am also an archaeologist. My name is Irene Saarni. I am Indian. I have lived in America. In Hawaii. Where are you from?"

"California."

"I have never been there. I am a friend of Jane's. She said you are very famous."

She wore a white lab coat, which looked out of place here in the midst of green grass and brick buildings. She seemed to struggle to repress nearly overpowering amusement. "I have my résumé here in this folder, if you want to see it, although there is no reason to believe everything written in a résumé."

They wandered into the student crush, a pub-cum-coffee shop. They found a corner, far from anyone who could possibly overhear them. Davis was fascinated by this strange, small woman. He glanced at her résumé. She had worked on a dig in Turkey, in the ancient city of Aphrodite. On the island of Kauai she had helped unearth a lava-brick aqueduct. She had received medical training as a pathologist at the University of London. Davis guessed that she had considered, at one time, pursuing a medical career. She had worked on the exhumations of ancient graves in London, and had written an article on the skulls of the Roman cemetery here in York.

"Where are you staying?" she asked.

"In a flat belonging to the Foundation, on Saint Mary's."

"I live exactly next door to you. Do you know how to preserve our Skeldergate Man?"

"In a general way."

"So you are knowledgeable on the subject of bog men?"

"I'm pretty well versed on the subject. I did work on the Tollund Man during my college years. I did a tour of Scandinavia. I've studied the Lindow Man, of course, although the fact that he was cut in two by a backhoe as they found him makes him seem—well—incomplete. He's Britain's favorite bog man. He's lying there in the British Museum, for all to see. I was a part of the team that contour-mapped him."

"And so your experience tells you how to proceed."

Her barely suppressed glee challenged Davis, in a way he found stimulating. She seemed to be interviewing him, and to find him very amusing. He toyed with the thought of being annoyed by her, but her eyes were too bright. "I have a pretty good idea," he said.

"Jane speaks very highly of you. She says I will learn a great deal working with you. I certainly hope so."

"You sound as though you don't believe it."

"I am a natural skeptic." She smiled. She had very white teeth, and as she mocked him, Davis found himself not knowing what, exactly, to say.

"I suppose you know all about the site," she continued. "All the things that people say about it."

"I have no idea what people say."

She laughed. "Then you will be very surprised. And you will not believe it. I think I should have you speak with my friend Mr. Foote. With an *e* at the end. He is a great scholar of this city. You will find him very interesting." She laughed again. "You have such a serious expression, Mr. Lowry. I think I will enjoy working with you very much."

* * *

That night they began to work on the Skeldergate Man.

Davis wore a shaggy wool sweater under his lab coat, and Irene wore a jacket under hers.

Davis was curious to see if her cheerfulness would continue in the face of this ancient death. The black sheet was whisked to one side, and the body bag was unzipped. The ebony sleeper was exposed, glistening, under the fluorescent light.

"He is a handsome fellow," said Irene.

"I want to do more C-fourteen dating. The reports of twelve hundred years give or take a few hundred are enough to satisfy the police."

"But they don't satisfy you."

"I want to send some bone to some people I know at the British Museum. I know people at Oxford, and they tend to destroy less tissue in the process, but Dr. Higg practically owns the British Museum. They'll give us the fastest results."

"And there you stand, Mr. Lowry, with your scalpel in your hand, not wanting to cut our friend."

It was true. Davis was stalling. He held the blade in his hand, and could not so much as touch it to the skin.

"I believe that five or six grams from the shin, and five or six from a hand, will be sufficient, Mr. Lowry. I will do it. The bone is so decalcified it is much like dried-out sponge. Here—this is enough femur. See how dry and porous it is. A Ziploc bag. Thank you."

"You do this well."

"You should not be surprised. I am cutting into the hand. I am sorry to do this, old friend. You are so handsome. But here—see how your metacarpals are like rotten wood. You have been dead a long time."

"There's a bag of some of the peat material found around the body," said Davis. "They'll want to test that, too."

"This is a cold room."

"Between four and six Celsius."

"He will keep well here. But I think we should apply water to him. He begins to dry out. We have distilled water here. That will do nicely."

"I took some tissue scrapes off his feet this morning. It's the only work I've had time to do so far. This is only my first entire day here in York." Why did he find himself wanting to apologize for not doing more? "I found two fungal organisms—penicillium and candida."

"I thought candida would be called a yeast organism, but I may be wrong."

"I can't recall."

She laughed. "And I can't either. And I can't recall if those organisms are a source of decay, or not. We don't want our poor fellow to have athlete's foot, do we?"

"They used to tan bog men," said Davis, "like leather, as a way of preserving them. That's the process nature began, anyway. They would tan them in a bark solution, rub them with oil—lanolin, or cod liver—and inject the saggy parts with collodion."

"I hope you don't suggest we do that to our friend. I know exactly what we should do with our ancient friend. We won't keep him like an old boot."

"I wasn't suggesting—"

"We will have him freeze-dried, like coffee. Like food for mountain climbers. We will soak him in something kind to him—polyethylene glycol and water, at fifteen percent—and then when he is dried out we can keep him at a normal temperature, and not in a giant refrigerator like this."

There was something mocking about her manner, insouciant, impenetrably happy. He was still slightly annoyed by her, but he was won over by her, too.

"But we are wasting time," she said. "Use your tape recorder. We must continue. I am ready." She set forth what Davis recognized as an endoscope, a metal tube for looking inside body cavities. She straightened a stainless steel tray on a side table. "Now, when you extract the gut, we will have somewhere to put it."

"We don't have to do everything in one night."

"We will want to know what was his last meal. Hurry, Mr. Lowry. For a famous man, you are very slow."

"I don't like to be rushed."

"You are standing like a statue. I cannot tell who is the bog man, the one standing up, or the one lying down. You are both too slow."

Davis found the ON switch on the Panasonic. He cleared his throat. "We have a remarkably preserved male of as yet imperfectly determined age. In general appearance he is well built. His shoulders

43

are fully muscled." He bent closer to the head. "The pinna of the left ear shows some loss of inner cartilage. Otherwise, there is no sign of decay or, for that matter, damage, except for a wound to the throat."

"Continue, Mr. Lowry."

"The hair of his head is reddish-to-ginger in color. Probably a postmortem change in pigmentation. Much of the body has lost calcium to the extent that the limbs are spongy-to-hollow in feel. Pending the results of a computerized axial tomography workup there is no way to determine the presence of a foreign body as possible cause of death. A xeroradiograph will help determine skull fractures, if any, and other such details impossible to observe from the outside."

He switched off the tape recorder.

"You are doing a magnificent job. Shall I insert the endoscope?"

He hesitated.

"I will make only a small hole. We want to look around the body cavity, Mr. Lowry."

"There is something very strange about all of this. Forgive me, Irene. I have to stop for a moment."

"It is too powerful, the presence of this ancient murder."

She said this calmly, even happily, but she looked into Davis's eyes, and seemed to understand him.

"Forgive me. I have trouble maintaining my professional detachment lately."

"You need not apologize. I am pleased to see that you understand our friend. He wants our respect. He will not mind if we study him. If we are respectful of the dead, they will not harm us."

Davis laughed, but she did not laugh in return.

The Skeldergate Man seemed to barely sleep. He seemed to twitch and toss, uneasily, in a dream.

As if he had made a sound.

Davis glanced up, to see if Irene had heard it.

She smiled back at him expectantly. "We can continue," she said.

The hand of the Man moved. It was only unfolding, Davis saw, from an awkward position.

It continued to move.

Davis held his breath until it stopped.

44

6

Davis and Jane reached the pub before anyone else. They each arrived at the same time by purest coincidence. They sat in the corner, beside the fireplace. Davis bought them both a pint of Stone's, and Jane told him about the accident in Trench Five.

"Oliver looked dead. We all were certain that he was, really, and then he came back to life. Peter was the one responsible, actually. He always seems to know what to do in an emergency."

"Have there been an unusual number of accidents at the site?"

"There's no question about that at all. I've never seen so many accidents, most of them, I hasten to add, entirely unexciting."

"Is there—I want to put this correctly. Is there talk about the site?"

"Talk?"

"I don't even know how to ask this. Is there a certain amount of superstition regarding the site?"

"I'm the last person to know about such things. There may be, among the wage earners, the laboring men, and such. I certainly haven't heard anything."

"Tell me what you know about Irene."

Jane tilted her head and studied him for a moment. "I just spoke to Irene."

"Yes?" Davis prompted.

"I had already told her everything I knew about you. Which is not, I must say, very much. But she asked me for more information, and I really didn't know quite what to tell her. She said you were a very interesting man."

Davis was surprised how happy this bit of news made him. He felt—and this bewildered him—as though he were blushing.

"Because you are, I have to agree, an interesting man."

"I'm beginning to feel embarrassed."

"I would have thought you accustomed to all sorts of flattery."

But this was more than flattery. Jane was, in her somewhat suave, even formal way, making a play for Davis. It was unmistakable. The sideways looks, the accidental, not accidental touching of his wrist with her hand.

Peter knew as soon as he saw the two of them what was happening. Davis had the stupid look on his face, pleasured and self-conscious. And Jane had as close to a come-hither look as she could have managed anywhere outside an actual bedroom.

But before he could absorb any of this, the rest of the crew arrived, even Langton.

Langton was notoriously stingy. He ordered the pints of bitter, and had Skip bring them over to the round tables. Everyone was buzzing with the story of Oliver, who had just been released from York District Hospital. Oliver beamed, delighted to be the dead man who woke up. As Skip told it, the accident had been the funniest event in years. "The place chews people up and spits them out, doesn't it, Oliver?"

"It chewed us up, all right."

So that's the way it's going to be, thought Peter.

"Here's to all of you hard workers for all the work you have been doing, and, I'm sure, will continue to do." Langton raised his pint.

The dozen or so laborers and scientists lifted their glasses, and drank. The bitter tasted like dirty dishwater to Peter.

"You're all right, aren't you, Peter?" asked Mandy.

"Why shouldn't I be?"

46

"Of course he's fine," said Skip. "Enjoying the great hospitality of Mr. Langton. We're all together, and Mr. Langton wants us to drink our fill tonight, I can tell that."

Langton beamed nervously. "I thought a pint after work—"

"A pint or two or three after work, said Mr. Langton to himself, and here we all are, thirsty as the Gobi, every last one of us." Skip gave Peter and Mandy a wink. "So drink up, all, and here's our gratitude to the bounty of Mr. Langton."

"Whatever is the matter now, Peter?" asked Mandy softly.

"Nothing," snapped Peter. "Everything is fine."

First Margaret. Now Jane.

Langton was smiling very unhappily. Skip had drained his pint, and held up his empty glass like a trophy. Davis and Jane drained theirs. Then there were empty glasses all around. Skip continued his toast, praising Mr. Langton, the most generous employer, the drinking man's friend. Alf joined in, raising an empty glass with an arm that was blue with tattoos.

Langton dug out his wallet and climbed to his feet with the expression of a man being punished.

Peter drank. The feeling would not go away, that rock in his stomach. It was a leaden lump, and it would not dissolve. Margaret and now Jane. And to think he had considered for a few days that he and Davis could work together. What a fool he had been.

It was much later. Nearly all the Skeldergate team had gone. Alf stopped by Peter's table and congratulated all of them, including himself, on getting Langton to buy a drink or two for once. "I think he hated doing it, too," said Alf. He left, waving a snake-decorated arm as he departed into the night.

Peter slouched in a corner. He had switched from bitter, but the Bell's whiskey had taken no effect, except to make the coins he used to pay for the drink seem heavy, and coated with grease.

Only Skip and Oliver remained of his team, although the pub was crowded, and hazy with smoke. Skip was waggling a finger in the face of a man with huge triceps and biceps. Peter had seen this man unloading carts of swedes and turnips at the market. The swede carrier did not agree with the fine points of what Skip was saying. Oliver glanced from one surly face to another.

Davis deserved to be taught some sort of lesson, thought Peter

47

heavily. Some sort of very definite lesson. Peter had worked his way up, out of Leeds, beginning as a boy in the cellar at Marks & Spencer, stacking boxes and working so hard his back hurt. He had always been thin. But he mustn't remember those terrible times. Those very bad times. Those were finished forever.

He had grown into an accent that he even, at times, could be proud of. He wasn't one of these California scientists who get their faces in the magazines. His father had been a newsagent and a hard worker, quick and polite to every stranger, and his mother had lived in America for a time, typing for an insurance company. Good people, nothing to be ashamed of, ambitious, but not the background most scientists have. Davis didn't have a crooked tooth in his mouth. They were all straight and even possibly capped.

You don't have to worry anymore, the doctor had said. The future is yours. The past is far away.

There was a sound of unmistakably foul language coming from Skip's direction.

Just as it happened, Oliver caught Peter's eye from across the room. Peter struggled past the table before him, and reached Skip just as he pushed the crate lifter, and the crate lifter pushed back.

Skip bellowed. Peter and Oliver together manhandled Skip out of the pub, into the cold night.

"I've left my coat!" cried Skip. "You can't expect me to wander around without my coat in this freezing weather, can you?"

Oliver darted back into the pub for Skip's coat. As Peter opened his mouth to utter soothing small talk, Skip swore and threw a wide, arcing left hook at a figure lurching from the pub.

The punch connected. Bodies grappled. Peter seized Skip's leg, and dragged him out of the knot. Oliver joined him, and the two warriors panted, held apart by their mates.

Blood glittered on the pavement, blue in the glare of the streetlight.

"You can't fucking drink without fucking fighting, can you?" said Oliver, dragging Skip up into the dark. "If it wasn't for Peter and myself you'd have the fucking police. Best give me a hand with him, Peter, if you would, he's bloody-minded, and that's all there is to it."

Skip swore and muttered, but went along between the two of them.

"Fucking heavyweight champion," said Oliver.

48

There was a bitter north wind, and they had to walk all the way to Burton Stone Lane. By the time they had reached Skip's flat he was furious at himself, and hitting himself great punches in the head.

"Easy, now, Skip," said Oliver. "You're pissed and you got into a bit of a fight, but you don't have to go pounding yourself in the skull."

Skip calmed himself. "I'm just at this turning here. You won't leave me, will you? I'll give you a drink and gratitude. You'll accept my hospitality, won't you, Peter?" said Skip. "You're an archaeologist." He said this the way he would have said, You're a hero. "A man who doesn't mind getting a bit of dirt under his nails and all that. Not like that mousy little man Langton. That man shudders at a fart, and that's the truth."

Peter sat in a kitchen crowded with dirty dishes and sports tabloids. The three drank gin out of teacups. "It's a haunted place, innit, that place?" said Skip. "For those as got a superstitious turn to them."

"The site?" said Peter.

"I don't know much about spirits myself. I just do the work. And I don't believe in spirits, myself, and nobody around there does. But we all know there's something peculiar about the place, don't we?"

"But it doesn't bother us a bit," said Oliver. "Not even a very little bit."

"That's right," said Skip. "We aren't afraid."

The cold cured Peter of the effects of the gin. The lights were turned off the Minster, and it was a great black hole where no stars glittered.

The stairs were dark. It was an effort, he supposed, to save electricity. He reached the door to his flat and found the key.

But the dark was not perfect. There was a light from the flat above. From under Davis's door. Davis's flat. Davis. The thought of him made Peter cold.

He was up there now, with Jane.

Davis tossed, breathing hard in his sleep.

The lake again. The water was calm, and barely shrugged in a light wind. For some reason the lake was larger now, and the figure of Margaret so much farther away. He called to her, calling her name.

She was farther away, and this meant that she was receding from him, and that day by day she would grow farther away until he couldn't see her again.

He called her name, weeping. Come back, he called, come back to me.

She came fast. Her body swelled from a distant dot, sweeping across the water, and was nearly upon him, the flesh flaking from her face as she came, exposing the blackened skull.

7

He woke with a start, and climbed to his feet. He leaned against the door frame, panting.

At least he was alone, with no one to see him like this. And at least he had not been sleepwalking. He slouched into the kitchen. He had left the light on. He switched it off, and the stillness of winter York lay before him. Frost had breathed on the slate roofs, and he found himself counting the chimneys he could see in the starlight. Fifty, and more.

The night went badly. He was afraid to sleep, but when he slept he was more afraid to dream. He woke several times, and listened to his Walkman, but there were no British stations that he could find, except one which played very much out-of-date pop tunes. He did find a German station, and listened to it, and a strange fluttering station he could not identify. Was it Farsi? He had learned a little of that elaborate tongue once, before the opportunity to conduct digs in Iran dwindled to nothing. The station was too far away, although it was more pleasant to stare into the dark listening for distant voices than it was to sleep.

He had not left it all behind.

It had come with him. Or, more correctly—she had come with him.

She was there, beside the lake, waiting.

Jane had the perfect voice, soft, very London, very BBC. So she did most of the talking.

They sat in a radio studio, not far from St. Andrews College. Jane was explaining that the Skeldergate Man would turn out to be a much more important find than any of the other bog men ever discovered. "Such a really marvelous opportunity to discover what, for example, the diet of the British people of that time period might have been."

"And how, exactly, is this sort of information actually gathered?" The interviewer had a list of questions before him, and he ticked them off as they were answered.

"The gastrointestinal tract, of course," said Jane, as though the question had been slightly rude.

"Very careful examinations of the seeds remnant in the lower intestine, Mr. Walker," said Irene.

Davis smiled to himself. Irene's accent was a sort of singsong, her words alternating very high or very low. He loved listening to her, and was lost for a moment when a question was directed to him.

"There are other ways," Davis began, "to determine the age of the body, aside from carbon-fourteen dating, which is not all that precise. We can use follicle erosion as a test—how badly decayed the hair is. We can try to recapture blood from the body cavity, and judge the rate of its disintegration. The blood in such bog men is long since decayed into a sort of black glue." This was certainly going to give the listeners of Yorkshire radio some meaty information to accompany their lunchtime toad-in-the-hole. "I'm not sure we can count on blood samples as a source of information in this case."

In the engineer's booth, a man with earphones sat with his eyes closed, drawing on a cigarette. The table at Davis's fingers was carpeted. The host, a pale man with a sparse mustache, seemed at once eager to know everything and slightly horrified.

"Most such men are found in actual peat bogs," said Jane, in answer to another question, which was, as she spoke, ticked. "But this particular body was deposited in a well lined with oak planks, much of it still having bark attached to it. The conditions had the same results, really, but in a way much superior to the usual peat-induced preservation."

"Of course," said Walker, "we all want to know everything about this man. How he lived, and how he died. We understand that you have a feeling this man may have been murdered."

"Killed, certainly," said Jane. "We can't rule out human sacrifice, although I doubt that was quite as popular in late Anglo-Saxon Britain as it was in much earlier times."

"But at the end of the day you do, I hope, intend to find out what exactly caused the Skeldergate Man to die."

"Of course," said Jane. "We should be able to find out everything there is to know about him, although it will take a good deal of time. And, of course, since our research is not government supported in any way, the public should be aware of the great costs involved."

Clever Jane. She knew why Dr. Higg wanted as much publicity as possible. "Remember to mention donations from the public," Langton pleaded in the waiting room.

"I think that we can very easily exaggerate the powers of science in the face of such mysteries," said Irene in response to no question at all. "I think there are things we will never know about our friend. How he died, and who he was, may forever elude us."

"But I think," said Jane, "we can all agree that we will know a good deal more if the public can step forward—"

"Of course," Irene smiled, "the public will respond with great interest. It is an opportunity to see someone from another age, but more important than that it is an opportunity to see the ultimate taboo set before their eyes, because the dead are the last secrets in our world, now that the vagina is no longer unseen in public life. It is not too facile to say that death is the most potent pornography, not, of course, for its sexual content, but because it is that which we are not supposed to see."

"This is fascinating," began Walker.

"I don't think you can assign," Jane responded with the sweetest of voices, "any degree of prurience to a public interest in such matters."

"Nor could I suggest," said Irene, plainly delighted with the discussion, "that any interest in the vagina is at all unhealthy, from any viewpoint. I was making a simple observation, quite aside from what anyone else might think."

"A personal observation," said Jane just slightly less sweetly, "not supported by any general view shared by the rest of the staff."

"Of course it's my own view," laughed Irene. "We do not all sit around the Foundation discussing the vagina."

Small points of red starred Jane's cheeks. "Surely you have more important questions, Mr. Walker."

Walker was concerned, plainly, at the turn the interview had taken, but was enough of a professional to know a potential debate when he heard it. "Let me see if I can reword Miss Saarni's fascinating observations," he said.

"Yes," said Davis. "I think it's a point well worth considering."

Jane destroyed Walker with a glance, and carefully ignored Davis. "We hope to know to what class this gentleman belonged, and perhaps to even know more about the murder itself."

"Yes," said Walker, shakily. "But tell me, Miss Saarni, do you believe our interest in death is healthy or unhealthy?" He did not tick this question. He had set aside his list.

"Only quite human, Mr. Walker. It is the last mystery for so many of us, the one aspect of human life which we cannot fathom, and while I do not want to belabor the subject of pornography, with all its distasteful implications, particularly for women, I do believe there is something more than rational, or less, in our interest in such an old corpse as this."

Davis listened, enchanted.

Jane folded her arms, and gazed straight ahead.

When they emerged into the waiting room, Langton was ashen.

"He will be calm after a few days," said Irene. "You, Davis, should have more faith in people."

They were walking the city walls. To their right was the great citadel of the Minster. Davis marveled at Irene's confidence. "I wonder if you ever make a mistake," he said.

"I do not concern myself with mistakes. Where people are concerned I am usually right."

"Why not be sure of yourself? Why not say that you're always right?"

"You, Davis, for example. You are so serious all the time. You

54

think life is something for work and thinking. Sometimes you should rest. You should do something you enjoy."

"I'm enjoying this," said Davis, before he could stop himself. And then he was glad he had said it. It was true. He was enjoying walking here on the walls of York with this fascinating woman. He was holding her hand, to his surprise. He could not remember who had made the first move. It had happened as though the two hands had minds of their own, and had sought each other.

Walking the walls like this it was impossible to think that anything bad had ever happened. "Tonight," said Davis, "will be an important night in the history of England."

"Tell me what will happen."

"Tonight we will explore the pubs of York. If you feel up to it."

"If I feel up to it! Davis, you are such a silly man."

That night, Davis and Irene started their pub exploration in The Hind, a pub on Blossom Street. Then they wandered farther, to Mount Vale, where there was a pub called Red Lion with loud music and bitter brewed in Tadcaster. Yet another pub was more quiet, with potted plants and a fire in the fireplace.

A man with red cheeks told them that a vixen had bit the leg off his cat.

"So they have foxes in Bolton Percy?" asked the man's companion.

"Oh, aye, foxes at the very least."

"What color foxes, I wonder," said his companion.

"Oh, the usual color."

"Pink, are they? Like the elephants."

"But the poor cat," said Irene. "To lose its leg."

"It was five years ago, love," said the red-faced man. "The cat runs better on three legs now than I do on two."

"This is a sad story, then," said the man's companion.

When they were alone in a corner of the pub, Irene was radiant. "To frighten us with a story that happened five years ago. I thought it was something that happened yesterday."

But she was not simply relieved about the cat's good health. She had something in mind. "Do you want to see the foxes hunt rabbits, Davis?"

"Of course. I don't think I've ever seen anything like that."

55

"I can show you where they hunt rabbits. Tonight, if you want to see."

They drank another pint, and then ventured out into the cold. It was a good chill. Davis put his arm around her, just slightly unsteady with the surprisingly strong beer.

"Are you sure," said Davis, "that there are foxes at night?"

"Of course, Davis, and rabbits, too. You know so little."

Davis admitted that this was true.

"You would rather stay inside, would you, and not see the rabbits and the foxes?"

Davis would go anywhere she went, and said so.

It was a long walk, and Davis, who had been partly refreshed by the cold wind, now found himself lost. The Terry chocolate factory loomed in the distance, far to the east. They walked purposefully across a field.

She held his hand and would not let him leave the path.

"Why not?" said Davis. "It's just a field, isn't it?"

"Bad things happen to people who wander," said Irene cheerfully.

They reached a small hill, and sat.

"Here," said Irene. "Here—if we sit still, we can hear them bark."

They were warm together, when he held her. Then Davis heard them. Distant clicks, like small sticks breaking.

"Foxes," breathed Irene.

"Really?" said Davis. He was amazed. He had never heard a fox before now.

But then there was silence.

A long silence. Davis turned his head one way, and then another, but he could hear nothing.

"I frightened them away," said Davis.

She did not speak at once. "Davis, I have something terrible to tell you."

"What?"

"I made it all up, about the foxes. I only wanted to get you out here, in the beautiful field, in the dark."

"You mean—there are no foxes at all?"

"Of course there are foxes. But the ones I talked about were pretend."

She was warm when he held her. "What made the clicks?" he asked at last.

"There was nothing, Davis. You heard them in your mind."

Davis insisted. "I want to find out what made the noise."

The night was very dark, and he collided with it before he could see it. It turned slowly and shook its head, violently, and he heard the clicks of its halter.

He led it back, and it followed, huge and warm in the dark.

For once Irene was surprised. "You found the biggest rabbit in the world," she laughed.

"It's a fox," Davis replied.

The horse nuzzled him, with gusts of warm air from its nostrils.

Long after they had left it Irene was still laughing, and Davis was still stopping to look back toward the place where the horse stood, invisibly, in the darkness.

8

Oliver, redheaded and sweating, was attacking a stump of concrete in the side of Trench Three. A graduate student, a pale, pudgy young man with glasses, was scraping the surface of the trench floor. He was scraping in the approved manner, always in one direction, a small ridge of scrapings always before him, until it became a crest, and could be dumped carefully into a black bucket.

Peter had spent the morning repairing the generator. The repair had been simple. A belt had broken. Belts are made to be broken, and Peter had kept a spare in the tools department, but the spare was missing. An auto supply shop on Bootham had every kind of belt but the one he needed. At last, a shop in Fulford had a used belt, and Peter brought it back to the site, carrying it to the generator like a prize eel.

Now the generator rumbled pleasantly. The office lights were on, and Peter sat in the Portakabin, wiping his hands on the old Mickey Mouse T-shirt he kept for such purposes. He watched Oliver through the window as he crunched the dagger end of the mattock into the stump of concrete. Bits of concrete flew.

Oliver was a wiry man, long recovered from his minor concussion. For a lean man, he was very strong. Concrete burst through the air, and sweat gleamed on Oliver's arms.

Time stopped. The head of the mattock detached itself from the shaft. It seemed to will itself upward, spinning, a tight blur that looked too small to be a great span of iron. Peter parted his lips, but he could not cry out. He could not move. He could do nothing.

The spinning iron reached the apex of its flight, and seemed to hover. It rolled over, as though to view the scene below, deliberately. It was this apparent deliberateness that froze Peter. The mattock head adjusted the angle of its fall, did one slow cartwheel, and then it fell straight to the head of the graduate student. There was a sickening crack—a quiet crack, bone and iron.

The young man sagged forward, and for an instant looked like someone demonstrating the myth of the ostrich. Then he fell sideways, and his eyes were open.

Peter leaped down the steps, ran to the edge of the pit, and jumped. He fell much longer than he had expected to fall, but he had no thought for himself, or for his body. He sprawled when he landed, and scrambled, calling to Oliver, "Lift his legs!"

Peter searched for a pulse. There was nothing.

"Good God in heaven," murmured Oliver. He held the man's feet, one under each arm.

"Where's his helmet?" muttered Peter. But it was obvious where it was. It lay at the foot of the ladder, beside the young man's coat, which he had carefully folded.

"I called for an ambulance," cried Jane, far above.

"Wake up," said Peter, putting his lips beside the young man's ear. "Wake up. We're all with you. Wake up—everything will be all right."

He was talking to a dead man.

Peter gave him the kiss of life, working with trembling hands.

There was no pulse. The eyes stared. Peter's breath filled the lungs, and wheezed out of them, again and again. An ambulance wended from the east. The high-low, one-two of its call seemed to grow farther away at times. Time was not standing still, now. It was moving in jerks.

"Wake up," called Peter. "Please wake up."

"Dear God in heaven," said Oliver.

Afterward, Peter would relive this moment time and time

59

again. His hands were on the young man's throat, this inert flesh, realizing he didn't even know the name of this young volunteer. The eyes were still open, and the lips were gray.

And then the eyes closed. A corpse, and the eyes closed. Peter straightened, unable to believe what he was seeing.

The body laughed.

A dead body, laughing. A chuckle, really, and a derisive one. Oliver dropped the legs.

Both men watched as the body stirred. The eyes opened, and the whites clouded from flushed pink to bruise gray to black. The lips darkened to gray, and then, as both men held their breath, the lips, too, were black. The corpse seemed to stare at both of them with eyes that were black holes.

And then it laughed, an ugly, husky sound, like the baying of an ancient dog. The body shuddered, arms shivering, legs twitching. There was a single inhaled breath, an intake of air so hard it was nearly a scream. Its chest rose and fell, in jerks.

Peter sank to his knees, wondering what lay before him. The young man's lips began to color again, from eggshell blue to flesh pink. Peter put his hands on the young man's chest.

The whites of his eyes were a normal color again, and the eyes were blinking. A tremor passed through his arms. His lips parted. His broken voice asked, "What happened?"

"You'll be fine," said Peter.

"You were dead," said Oliver. "But you came back to life." He looked at Peter. "Didn't he?"

Peter didn't answer.

But the broken voice stayed with Peter as he surveyed the trench. The ambulance had come and gone, and Peter was thankful to have the world return to its rubble and mud. Muck and rock: this was what he understood.

But what had happened? There had been a dead body here in the trench, killed by a violent accident. It had died and returned to life. More than that, the mattock head had seemed to move on its own, purposefully.

Then his questions evaporated. Peter laughed. It was all, in a way, a bad joke. And, if one really thought about it, a fairly funny joke. This was not going to soothe the nervous workers. This was not going to help anyone work more calmly. This was not going to help Davis either. This was not going to help the grieving American sleep better at night.

Because as he gazed at the empty trench, and at the head of the mattock as it lay in a puddle, Peter understood something. He understood how much he hated Davis. It was as though a genius of hatred blossomed within him, and he could see clearly all that had been a blur before now.

He was going to make Davis regret coming back to York. He was going to frighten Davis, very badly. He was going to destroy Davis's sanity.

And then, Peter promised himself, there would be that most delicious task, a goal worth struggling to achieve. It would be entertaining. It would be great sport.

He would not simply murder him—that would be too simple. He would frighten Davis out of his mind, and then, with the ease of a man controlling a distant airplane, he would destroy the man he hated above all else in the world.

Even then, Peter tried to shake away this great hunger. Was it, he thought, just, really? Wasn't it a return to the old times, those old, buried nights, when he thought only of killing?

Don't do it, he tried to tell himself, actually speaking the words through his teeth.

Don't do it. Don't kill him.

9

Irene's new computer had arrived, and Davis dropped by in the evening to see it. Her flat was in the bottom of the building next to his, and it was a single very large room with a very small kitchen. They sat, drinking tea, and from time to time a person walked by above on the sidewalk, a flash of pant legs or the glitter of a dog chain.

"I have already set up my computer, Davis. I did not need your help."

"I didn't assume you needed help. I was curious. I like working with computers."

"Now I will be able to write my articles. I am contributing editor to two journals, Davis. I am very busy, you see, and do not often entertain a gentleman like this. In fact, I am very slightly embarrassed and I shall close the curtain—help me, please—lest people look down at us and think what people might well think." She laughed when the curtain snagged and would not close at once.

"You are so continually happy that at times I resent you," said Davis.

"It is because of your troubles, and your grief. You see me happy and you think I am detestable."

"Not detestable. In fact, I don't know very much about you."

"My résumé is all entirely accurate. If you read that carefully, then you know everything important about me."

"Even now, I think you are joking. You are incorrigibly flippant."

"I am sorry I trouble you."

"You aren't sorry at all."

"No, indeed, although I am sorry that you have such deep sorrows, Davis, and that is the truth."

"If I could see you spend an hour without laughing at something."

"No, you mean if I could spend an hour without laughing at you."

To his surprise Davis found himself unable to take his eyes off hers.

"You think I am mocking you every time I laugh. Perhaps the source of my pleasure is quite unimaginable to you."

"Perhaps."

"Perhaps I find joy in your presence, Davis, and that is something you have not considered."

Her lips, when he brushed them with his, tasted of cloves. He had not intended to kiss her, and in fact as soon as his lips touched hers, he backed away, and then found himself not backing away at all.

She was a person who never wasted a movement, or a moment. She put her fingers to his lips, although Davis was not about to speak, and had nothing to say. She smiled up at him, as though challenging him, but there was nothing mocking about her now.

She was slender. Her clothes lay on the floor, but she had cast them down so gracefully, for all the quickness of her movements, that they looked like dancing, abstract figures.

He had not held a woman, or really desired one, ever since that terrible day. He had, he realized, surrendered to the possibility of never feeling this way again.

"So, you see," she said at last, when they lay drowsily in the semidarkness, "you are able to feel happiness, and to give it, after all."

He was silent for a while. "I wonder if you can read my mind," he whispered, not wanting to break a mood that amazed him. He would have been unable to name his feeling. It was a happiness that he had, without knowing it, believed he would never experience after Margaret's death.

"I can read your feelings, Davis," she said. "It is very easy to do."

"Then," he whispered, "you must know how happy I am."

She laughed, a low, loving laugh. "You will have much happiness in your life, Davis. You should not be afraid."

Much later, when they woke, he asked her, "Aren't you ever sad?"

"You know that I must be sad sometimes, Davis. I have seen good people die."

Davis felt a twinge of shame. Of course she must have mourned at times in her life, as everyone did. It was a part of the self-centered aspect of his grief. He had assumed that he was the only person who ever mourned.

"I come from a place where people die easily. There is always death."

"It must be terrible."

"I miss the egrets," said Irene. "Everywhere I have lived, there have been cattle egrets. They wait around the buffalo as they feed, watching for millipedes to scurry. Even in Hawaii, there have been those white birds. But here in England, there are no such birds."

"They have rooks," said Davis. He wondered what time it was, and sat up. "And crows."

"You must hate those birds," said Irene.

He sensed a return of her mockery. "Why should I hate them?"

"The rooks are always laughing," she said. "When you see a stand of trees, the great black birds are high in the branches, laughing and laughing, entertaining each other by their endless laughing. Davis, you would hate to be a rook. Do you think that nature is always sad? You must realize that sometimes it does nothing but laugh."

Davis fumbled.

"What are you looking for, Davis?"

"My watch."

She laughed. "Do you have an appointment in the middle of the night?"

He did not answer.

"And, furthermore, do you ordinarily remove your watch when you make love to a woman?"

"At least I amuse you," said Davis ruefully. "I've never known a woman who found me so endlessly entertaining."

"You are not only entertaining, Davis," she said, in a different timbre. "You are a delight to me."

He found her hand on his shoulder, and he found her pulling him down to her, and wanting him, opening herself, and he found himself forgetting everything that had ever happened to him, except this one room, and this bed.

10

Peter was at the dig early. He made a cup of Nescafé, and pried the lid off the bottle of milk he had brought from his flat. He believed in keeping milk and sugar and tea and such things in the main Portakabin. It made things cozy for the workers. He believed in tea breaks, and kept a big black kettle on the two-burner propane stove. He rolled one of his slim cigarettes, but it was difficult because it was a cold morning and his fingers were stiff.

His desk was a clutter of notebooks for his personal site journals, and for ideas that came to him in a flash. He had experienced several exciting ideas recently, and scrawled them in his spiral notebooks. He also kept a Munsell soil chart on his desk, and context cards for noting finds. There was also, often ignored, a yellow RMJ plastic helmet, made in England to protect the head of the absent-minded.

The poplar trees were like coarse, black feathers standing against a perfect gray sky, a sky as flat as a sheet of paper. It would snow, he thought.

Peter generally did not need much sleep. This was a good thing. He had been at York District Hospital until late the night before. Dr. Hall, the freckled physician, was, it seemed, an expert neurosurgeon. He had examined the young man, a gifted student in history. The student had been entirely lucid and reassured Peter that he still wanted to pursue archaeology. "Although, perhaps, at a different dig."

There was, Dr. Hall reported, nothing wrong with the young man.

"You're quite sure?" Peter had asked.

"There's very little evidence of even a slight concussion. Why—what happened?"

"We gave him a helmet, but, for some reason, he decided not to wear it."

There had been the telephone calls with Langton, and with Dr. Higg. It was all very annoying, and although the event itself had been chilling, now Peter felt only sick of bureaucrats and their many questions.

It was easy to understand why someone might choose not to wear a helmet. They were always slipping down and blocking vision, and Peter often wore his backward, to avoid that problem.

Jane was always at the dig very early. She wanted to be professional in every way. Peter wondered if this had attracted her to him—the fact that he had, after all, some small reputation as a professional archaeologist, including a very recent article on Roman walls in St. Albans. Some of the walls had been painted to resemble stone, a motif well in keeping with modern Britain, in which heaters were decorated with plastic coals.

But the chat he wanted to have with Jane now was not professional, and it was not pleasant. Perhaps it was not even wise to have it here, but Peter, for the moment, did not feel like being wise.

Even so, he looked forward to seeing her.

The generator started, and the padlock on the toolshed surrendered after a few strong tugs. The inner workings of that particular lock always froze in the slightest cold.

Last night, when he had left, the tools had been lined up tidily, and the yellow helmets stacked, one on top of the other, in a column.

So many mornings he had arrived to see the tools in a jumble. Traffic vibration, Jane had suggested. The wind, suggested Mandy. Perhaps we don't leave them all that tidy after all, Langton had once offered.

They had been tidy last night.

Peter wrenched open the door.

67

The tools were a tangle. The helmets were strewn about the interior. Peter cursed. He didn't care what caused the mattocks to dance with the trowels anymore. The mystery, and it was a deep one, did not interest him at this moment. He had something more important on his mind.

It was not going to be a perfect day for work, but no one on the team would be reluctant to stand in the groundwater. They were a tough lot, even though some of the groundwater might well be frozen and have to be pried out with a shovel, like chocolate ice cream.

Jane was a round figure with all of her clothing, including a very long gray wool muffler. Her nose was pink, and she panted in the relative warmth of the Portakabin, beside Peter's desk, where a floor heater made a modest battle against the cold.

"Not very nice, is it?" Peter offered.

"It isn't," she said, running the words together so they sounded like *tisn't*.

He made her coffee.

"You're going to make this all very awkward for me, Peter." Something in Peter twitched.

"I don't think we should see each other anymore, for a while, at least." She would not look at him as she said this, and then she did. Right into his eyes. "I really think it's best."

Peter turned away. Muscles in his neck knotted.

"I think what we did that night was lovely, but it was also, I'm afraid, a mistake."

A beautiful night. Right after an Italian dinner and a walk up Dean Gate, right beside the Minster. Starlight through the naked trees.

Peter had expected a difficult moment with her. But the morning had vanished, and what was before him was a woman he loved, changed, in an instant, into a stranger. Her cheeks were pink. A lock of blond hair wandered. She had that too correct set to the jaw, and her eyes were cool. He saw it now. He had been right.

"You and Davis," he said in a low voice.

"I'm sorry?" she said, as though she had not heard him clearly, or did not understand.

"You and Davis," he said, very clearly.

"It's not true, Peter."

He knew it was true. He had seen them.

"I think, simply, that it's unprofessional to have a close relationship with a colleague, and while I am very fond of you— Please, Peter, don't make it more difficult."

Peter smiled. He knew this was not a pleasant smile. He would not make it difficult at all. He would make it very easy. He would make it all extremely easy for her. Because he did not blame her. He knew who was at fault. He had been a fool to think Davis and he might be able to work together. He would continue the charade, of course. Why let Davis know how much he was hated?

She was murmuring words about a continuing professional relationship. "I do so much value your friendship, and your expertise, Peter." She was ambitious, Peter knew, and knew how to succeed in a field that was thick with competition. No doubt this was a part of Davis's charm. The celebrity archaeologist, whose bed was one of the quickest paths to a bright future. He had promised her a chair at a university in California, a future of book signings and cocktails in exotic places. Even Jane, with all her confidence, was having trouble continuing. Her voice faltered. "If you could at least make some sort of effort to understand...."

Peter turned to her, and he used his best manner. "Of course," he said. "I understand perfectly what has happened."

He left, and found the heaviest hammer in the shed— "the giant-killer" he called it in his imagination. It was a great iron fist at the end of a shaft of wood. He stalked to Trench Nine, which had just been clawed open by the heavy equipment the week before. It was still a jumble of concrete and chunks of lumber, nineteenth-century warehouse beams.

Peter flung himself into the pit. The voices of workers reached him. They were just arriving. One of the men laughed, another whistled. The air compressor that worked the pneumatic drill coughed and started up. The site was all business now.

Peter used the great hammer, the giant-killer, on a chunk of concrete the size of a man. Concrete exploded. Peter grunted, and swung. And as he worked, something fluttered in his head, that sound he had hoped he had left far behind him, in the wet nights of his youth.

But he welcomed the sound now. Let it come—let it all come back. The old, terrible times had been life itself. He had been a fool to try to forgive Davis. He had been a fool to beg himself to spare Davis's life. He had been right all along. Davis was a trespasser, a greedy interloper, a man who took whatever he wanted, unthinking, uncaring.

Peter would smile and seem to be thinking of soil samples and finds notations. No one would be able to tell what he was thinking. What is the face but the most perfect, living mask?

Peter swung the hammer. It made the most solid, delicious sound, iron and concrete, and the concrete was beginning to surrender. It was beginning to crumble. It was powder.

A little boy's voice was speaking in his head. A soft, alert voice. "This has been a very, very naughty kitty, and it will have to be punished so awfully, awfully badly."

He would start with cats. He had always loved that. A man who can beguile a cat, deceiving the most cautious creature of the night, could deceive anything. Or anyone. And a cat was much like Davis. Self-assured, self-confident, arrogant to the point of making a fatal blunder.

But he was out of practice. He would have to sharpen his powers. It would be like the old times, when he had felt pleasure like nothing his adult life had given him. Why had he waited so long?

The concrete was demolished. It lay scattered at his feet. He let the hammer fall, and leaned, panting, against the wall of the trench.

First, cats. And then the man.

11

They were late getting to the lab, and hurried past the Minster in the cold. The wind was from the northeast, and carried with it the smell of chocolate from the Rowntree factory outside of town.

"The English fully understand that they cannot cook," said Irene. "Although this is unkind. A delicious bowl of trifle is very enjoyable, but the English suffer by being so close to France. People naturally think that Yorkshire pudding is not puffed pastry, and therefore is not good. The English have very cleverly and wisely elected to dine at their many Indian restaurants. They call them tandoori restaurants, but not all of them have a tandoori oven, which is a kind of clay barbecue."

Irene was hurrying ahead of Davis, but Davis was eager to hear her. He loved her voice, and the tireless amusement in her eyes. She seemed to find her opinions completely harmless. If Davis disagreed with her she would simply laugh and say, "Quite possibly."

She had spent the night with him. She had spent several nights with him, in his flat. The view of the Minster was, she said, delightful. "After a while, Davis, you will be unable to be sad."

He found himself thinking of her at odd moments, and now

that he was with her he did not want to miss a syllable. Her white lab coat fluttered behind her.

Langton had been forced to compliment her the day before. Her comments on the radio had tickled the public interest. Langton had received letters complimenting him on the insightfulness of his staff. Donations had increased fourfold.

Mandy met them. She was running, her cheeks flushed, and her size did not seem to have made her slow. She could not speak for a moment, catching her breath. "There's something wrong," she gasped.

Both Irene and Davis put their hands out to her, to comfort her.

"Something wrong," she repeated. "In the lab."

Their eyes were wide with questions.

"The Skeldergate Man," gasped Mandy.

They all ran. Keys did not seem to work, doors balked. Each door handle seemed to have frozen into place, and time moved with a granite slowness as Davis fumbled, inserted the wrong keys, and wrestled with doors.

At last, they were in the lab.

"I was bringing some finds trays down," said Mandy, still breathing heavily. "You see them there, right where they belong. And actually, although this isn't my favorite place, and never has been, I felt I should have a look round. Just a look. I don't know why. There was something wrong, I supposed, and I didn't know what."

The lab was, as always, cold. The lights above made their faint hum.

"And what happened?" asked Davis.

Mandy did not want to speak immediately. "I can't tell you."

Davis made a huff of impatience.

"You won't believe me," said Mandy. "But you'll see for yourself."

"I'll believe you—"

"I looked over at his room. Over there. And I saw that the door was open." Her voice trembled, and she took a breath. "And I thought why—how silly of someone to leave that door open like that. And I went over to the door to close it, and—"

Davis did not wait to hear her tell it. He hurried across the lab, and nudged the door to his room wider, and then he could not move.

He felt backward to the jamb for support. Mandy gasped behind him, and Irene slipped into the room and she, too, froze.

The Skeldergate Man was stripped of his plastic sheets. He lay on the floor, several steps from the table, and his hand was outstretched, reaching for the door.

"What," whispered Mandy, "happened to him?"

Davis felt the room pulse with his heartbeat. He cleared his throat. "He fell off the table."

"But—look at him," breathed Mandy.

"I only hope," said Davis, making himself sound as businesslike as possible, "that he isn't damaged."

Irene was thoughtful, but she knelt and touched his ginger hair, as though he were asleep before them, a drunk who had succumbed. "We must put him back."

Mandy fled.

12

"I'm afraid we are going to have real troubles on our hands," said Langton.

He and Dr. Higg waited for the light to change on the corner of Great Russell and Bloomsbury Streets in London. Langton had always felt very much the lieutenant to Dr. Higg, a smaller, less powerful version of the wiser man. He was comfortable with this role. Langton knew his own strengths. He had a good memory, and he did not mind work. But sometimes, just occasionally, he did not get on well with people, and sometimes his sense of humor failed him.

He had described things as they were in York, and Dr. Higg had suggested that they have a long chat here in London, and what better place to do it than in the British Museum, where Dr. Higg had his office? And yet it annoyed Langton just slightly to be called down to London, as though to be scolded by the headmaster, and to be taken to the museum, like a boy who had to be reminded that the business that absorbed them was of extreme importance.

But one of Langton's strengths was that he bore impatience well. He knew a superior man when he walked beside one, and Dr. Higg was that, in every way.

"Too many little mishaps," Langton continued. "Little bits here and there going wrong."

The light flashed a small green man. They hurried across the street, Dr. Higg striding just slightly in front, head forward in thought or determination.

"I thought, at first," said Langton, "that with Davis aboard much of it would be sorted out. But things haven't gone well, at all. I can't say they've gone worse, but they certainly haven't gone more smoothly, either."

A man was roasting chestnuts at the gate to the museum. He was burning them, actually, but the smell was delicious, a rich, charred scent nearly like seared beef. Guards nodded greeting to Dr. Higg, and he waved to them absentmindedly and grandly.

The real problem was something that Langton could not quite bring himself to address. He continued to nibble around the edges. "Of course, the site is extremely rich. I've never known a site to be such a treasure of finds and information. And the response to such discoveries as our Skeldergate Man is always very great."

"Is it," said Dr. Higg at last, "a matter of safety?"

"Only in the most general terms." Langton knew that this was a very incomplete answer, and that even Dr. Higg would grow impatient after a while. This was all a matter of his duty, Langton knew, but he really would rather be in York, where he always felt much happier. Langton understood York, and had always seen London as somehow un-English, a stew of Americans and Frenchmen, all with too much money. He wished, for a moment, he were in York, away from this traffic, watching his border collie sport in the marsh of Clifton Ing. But this was mere wishful thinking, and pointless. "Of course it is a matter of safety."

"There is something you are not quite telling me, Charles."

Langton did not respond.

"And I think I can imagine, in general terms, what it is."

Langton rather doubted this. He wondered, very briefly, if vanity was in fact an important part of the wiser man's makeup. Langton had been known, from time to time, to bet a pound on a horse or two. He would be willing to bet, now, that Dr. Higg could not guess what Langton's news was, when it was trimmed of all its dressing.

Langton decided to be as circumspect as possible. "Of course, the basic reason for your asking me to travel two hundred miles was no doubt to improve my own morale—"

"Our morale, Charles, is relatively unimportant. We are expendable. It is the morale of our warriors—our workers, our time-soldiers, I like to call them. That is all that matters."

They had entered Dr. Higg's office. Shelves were lined with tobacco-brown skulls, and plaster-yellow casts of skulls, and the sun-red gleam of gold buckles and pins. The desk itself was bare, except for a pen and blotter, but it was plain that Dr. Higg's interest was drawn to the walls around him, to the frame that held a span of Anglo-Saxon wool, and the row of Romano-British spearheads.

Dr. Higg asked Langton to sit, but wandered, for a moment, enjoying his collection. He brought a clay ring back to the desk, and held it in his hand as he considered what Langton had—and had not—told him. The ring was a loom weight, an object not unlike an American doughnut. It was heavy, and the clay was hard. He toyed with it, thinking how simple his life had become in recent years.

At one time he had lived a cluttered life, always leaving for Chicago or Mexico City. He had taught at York University and Stanford. He had given lectures in cities around the world—even, in slow English, at the University of Moscow—and he had sweated in the field in sites on every continent. He allowed himself one memory, because he did not like to look back, a characteristic perhaps ironic in a scholar dedicated to mankind's past. He was not sentimental. He was a realist when it came to himself. He allowed himself a moment to recall the stony beaches of Samos, and how he had swum into the sea until the meltimi, that brisk Greek summer wind, had blown salt into his eyes, and he'd had to turn back half blind, and in love with life. They had found a colossal head of Aphrodite, not far from the ancient ruined town of Kamiros. Even now, the remainder of that great statue slept somewhere, broken into boulders in the foundations of buildings, or lost in the olive groves, just below the surface of the earth.

Higg loved archaeology, and he loved the homeliest objects that men and women had made as much as he loved the royal golden baubles of Sutton Hoo. He kept his life simple. His wife had died five years before, and now all that existed for him was his science. He had this office, and he had his study in St. John's Wood, a nightly whiskey, and dreamless sleep.

But he knew the things that could go wrong during a dig. He

knew the footsteps a scientist dreams of at night, the unholy songs he hears in the abandoned tombs of Oaxaca, and the figures just shrinking from torchlight in the death corridors of Mitla. All creations of the imagination, he knew. But the imagination was everything. What was man, but a mammal which imagined the world?

"Tell me, Charles. Is there any rumor about among the workers, and among the scientists, that the dig might be—and I want to use the right word—haunted?"

Langton was visibly surprised. He was also secretly irritated. He had lost his private bet with himself. "This is what I wanted to tell you. I was afraid to mention it, really. It is so terribly irrational. . . ."

Higg ran his fingers over the ancient loom weight. He could feel the indentations of fingerprints that had been dust for fifteen hundred years. "You were right to tell me." He sighed. "I can't unmake my decisions. But perhaps I was wrong to send Davis there, a man so recently bereaved. If I had thought through the implications of having him work on an ancient corpse, I would have sent him to Paris, to work on the excavations at the Cluny Museum. They are uncovering more of the Roman baths there."

"Davis is doing reasonably well. No more disturbed, as far as I can tell, than anyone else. Besides, I don't think Davis is alone in feeling disturbed. The entire team is troubled, and I must point out that our friend Peter is—"

Higg would not finish Langton's sentence for him.

Langton finished manfully. "Our friend Peter is not doing well. He looks ill."

Higg looked away. Peter had always been the real risk. "So we have troubles."

"Of course, the local people have long thought of Skeldergate as haunted. It was a point of amusement, really. I remember running past the old warehouses there when I was a boy. But we never took it especially seriously, even as children. York has its haunted pubs, and haunted churches. We don't take them terribly seriously. But now, suddenly, even the most rational of our team seems troubled. It's all quite ridiculous, of course."

"No, Charles, it's irrational, but it's not ridiculous. We deal, after all, not only with gold and bits of iron, but also with the dead, and the dead are potent beings, if only in our minds. It is the mind that is so powerful it can raise the dead, if only in our dreams."

Langton smiled nervously, or perhaps with a show of interest he only half felt. Langton was an administrator, thought Higg. A good man. But he was not in love with his science as Higg was, as he had been since as a boy his father took him to Stonehenge, that ring of watchful stones in the midst of Salisbury plain. Some people have found them disappointing, those enigmatic ruins of a dead religion. The five-year-old Higg had found them, as he would find them today if he traveled there, as alive and exciting as a herd of phantom dinosaurs.

"You've done well, Charles. Thank you for coming to see me." Still, Higg had to be honest with himself. Langton was a good man, but he was also a terrible bore.

Langton smiled, flattered, no doubt, but then he leaned sideways in his chair and lifted his eyebrows. Surely, his body language said, you have more to say than that?

Yes, thought Higg. He had much more to say. Langton had, years ago, thought of joining the Foreign Office. What a disaster that would have been, thought Higg. Langton had a better touch with dogs than he did with people. It would be dismal to spend any time at all in his company, but he had little choice. "I'm coming with you," he said. "To York."

PART Two

13

In the dark the brick buildings were like empty black caverns. The streetlights were dim smudges. The stones of the pavement glistened, although it was not raining, and it had not been raining for hours. There were no stars.

It had not been like this for years. Peter didn't care. The voice in him was clear, and his penis was swollen at the sound of it. All he had to do was catch one of the naughty, naughty creatures.

He had a tin of Norwegian sardines, and he had all the patience of justice. How could he have forgotten how wonderful this was? A simple trick, a box propped on a stick, a long string, and a tin of sardines. Just like the days behind the tiny gardens, among the rubbish bins, those days the smiling doctors had assured him were gone forever.

He had seen one here before, a black-and-white one. You could tell what a creature like that is thinking, just by looking. You can see into its heart and see what evil little things, all the evil little things, it wants to do. Lick the private parts of women. Things like that, nasty, naughty things like that. It had been years since he had thought like this, and now it made him so hard to think about it.

Think of all the years of pleasure he had missed by forgetting all of this.

Naughty creature, you'll have to be punished very badly.

He sat in the darkest part of the alley behind Queen Anne's Road. Three nights of this and it hadn't worked. But it would. It always used to work, eventually. All he had to do was wait. Sometimes a door slammed and he froze. His box didn't look like a trap. It looked like a pile of rubbish children had been playing with, and in a way that was all it was, really.

Oh, please, sir, it's nothing, only a toy, like, to play with, like.

It was so cold. He had his thick, fur-lined gloves on, and three pairs of stockings, but it was still so cold. All a part of the game, though. A little cold to whet his appetite. He sat with his back to a brick wall, and he waited.

Oh no, sir, I wouldn't want to do anything to hurt a cat, sir.

Wind swayed nearly invisible clouds, dragged them away. Sometimes one star barely throbbed through the black, and then dissolved again. All the bedroom windows were black. Everyone was asleep. The city was empty. The trees in the dim streetlight were a tangle of dried veins. Nothing moved on the ground. Nothing moved in him, except blood to his lust that was so hard now it hurt.

Nasty creature. So naughty.

He drowsed, and woke. What a fool to nod off like this, after all these hours. What if it came now, with him asleep?

But it didn't. There was the box on its single stilt. There was the dark, all around. He was invisible here, but nothing came.

It wasn't coming tonight, either. It was never coming.

Then it was there.

After being not-there, it was like a trick, like something impossible. Just as simply as if he imagined it. There in the box, its haunches and tail protruding out, the white parts of it so white, the black like parts that weren't there. There was wind shaking the sky, and a dry leaf months old scratched the ground, and he pulled the string.

Oh no, sir, I wouldn't know anything about any hurt cats.

The box fell, and the cat backed away, and nearly escaped. It wore the box like a hat too large, and the box made a dragging sound as the cat pulled back. Peter lunged, and fell across the box. The cat made a cry—a low cry, a cry not like the sweet, begging call cats made, a low, deep, strange note, the song cats make when they know.

He slid the flat stiff cardboard under it. He taped the cardboard up the sides of the box, and then he could turn it over. He had done this all before, so many years ago. It was such a pleasure. Why had he waited so long?

He hurried with the cat struggling inside, punching the cardboard with its head. Such a naughty creature, doing such nasty things with your tongue, and we know all about it. We will show you what happens to such naughtiness when it is found out, and when it is caught. Such bad, bad nastiness—you won't get away with it anymore.

Out onto the great black emptiness of the football field beside the river, the town a stipple of lights, barely there, the river a quaking black nothing.

The hand peeled back the cardboard, and the head of the creature was out, like a snake, urgent and surging, a serpent of nastiness.

At arm's length—it must be like that, or the naughty creature will do harm. It can do such nasty harm, this terrible, terrible thing. The box fell away. Holding the cat out at arm's length, the leather gloves around the neck, and the strong sleeves, leather under the wool coat, all armor against not simply the cold.

The gloves squeezed the throat. The cat was a struggling blur. It clawed the sleeves with its hind legs, arched itself, swung itself around, nearly breaking its neck with its fight. So much fight. The eyes in the dim starlight bulging. The mouth with its fine white fangs open in a scream that became air.

The jerking body clawed the dark, urine and feces spurting. The eyes popped out, like beans borne from soil on their own sprouts. It was all over now, but the body didn't know it, fighting and clawing at nothing.

Until, swung by the tail, it spun and sailed through the air, into the deep wet nothing of the river.

14

Higg was pleased to be back in York. The Minster was, as always, a magnificent sight, and the city walls, on their steep green embankments, were, as always, a sight that improved him. He took a brisk tour of the city with Langton tagging along behind. It was barely cool, and this meant that spring was nearly here. He was perfectly comfortable in his dark blue Moss Brothers overcoat, years old and fitting better each year. He did have some doubts about his new Smith Brothers blackthorn, replacing a stick he had lost in the Arno the summer before. He had been watching the fishermen and had experienced a moment of such absorption it amounted to complete absentmindedness, although it was not a sign, he hoped, of age.

He had dropped the stick into the water by accident, and it had been lost. As a young man he had smoked a pipe, and had given up the habit because he had lost several perfectly fine Dunhills in much the same way.

He struck the Anglian Tower with his stick, tapped the fragment of Roman wall, and, with Langton clearing his throat and suggesting that they ought to hurry to Skeldergate, he wandered over to Saint Mary's Bishophill, Junior, and gazed upward at the Anglo-Saxon Tower, the sole Anglo-Saxon tower in York, and a lovely piece of work. Some of the stones were unmistakably Roman in origin. Somewhere in this general neighborhood there had been a Mithraic temple, and that single Roman sanctuary had furnished fabric for many churches. Higg insisted on slipping inside the church itself to see the arch made, undoubtedly, of good red Roman rock.

He was even more delighted to see the dig itself. They had made such progress. He put on a yellow helmet, and climbed up and down ladders. Davis was there, and Higg was always pleased to see Davis. Such a sturdy young man, and bright. He was sorry the man had suffered such sorrows, but the work did seem to be agreeing with him, after all. Peter, though, seemed drawn and abstracted, although he shook hands and made entirely appropriate comments about the pleasing warmth of the weather, considering the time of year.

"Before we have our meeting," Higg said, "I want to see everything. Come along, Davis. I have questions for you."

They left Langton behind. The man was a master of words and numbers. He had no legs for a genuine ramble. They crossed the Ouse Bridge, and made their way past the Minster, out Monk Bar, to the college. Higg enjoyed the walk, enjoyed the green grass—he loved everything about this town, and his science.

Davis was describing the results of the CAT scan on the Skeldergate Man. There was no sign of fracture, and no foreign body to indicate an arrowhead or other such weapon. The digestive tract had yielded the predictable sorts of residual matter—berry seeds and wheat, trace pollens, hawthorn, and, although Davis wasn't certain, perhaps rape seed.

"Let's hurry along," said Higg. "I've never actually met our distinguished guest, you know."

They had the Skeldergate Man behind a series of locks. The laboratory was as Higg remembered it. Sterile and functional, and quite cold—lovely.

Davis and Miss Saarni stood aside, and Higg strode into the brightly lit, smaller room at the end of the laboratory.

"He's magnificent, isn't he?" said Higg at last.

The body had the sheen of fine, well-worn saddle leather. "You've done well, I must say, both of you. Is the preservation nearly complete?"

"Virtually," said Davis. But Davis had begun acting just

slightly strangely. He was unusually silent. Miss Saarni, who, Higg knew from one meeting several months before, was usually quite ebullient, a truly charming girl, was also quiet.

"And how are things with you, my dear Miss Saarni? I know you've been essential here, with all your skills and with your ready wit. Speak quite plainly. Have there been any problems here?"

"We have not suffered any problems, Dr. Higg. We have been more than proud to work here on this marvelous discovery."

"Where is that wonderful joy I recall, Miss Saarni? And you, Davis. Good heavens, I remember a young man who would jump up and down at the sight of a Cretan fibula. Now, here you are, with the greatest bog man ever discovered in scientific history, and you look as though you've forgotten all your first-declension nouns."

"He moves," said Davis.

Higg gazed at Miss Saarni, and then back at Davis.

"He moves during the night," said Davis.

Higg stared.

"We have found him on the floor several mornings in a row," Davis said, "each time—" Davis stopped himself. "Each time a little closer to the door."

"He seems to be wanting to escape," said Miss Saarni. "Although where he intends to go, I have no idea. Everyone is talking about it, all the workers at the dig. It only conforms to what everyone has thought for a long time. That the dig, and all associated with it, is haunted. I find it really quite unbelievable, naturally," she laughed. "But we have a good many physical phenomena that require explanation."

Her eyes were bright with something like humor, and for once Higg wished she did not have such a bubbling personality after all.

Higg gazed down at the ebony bog man. "Yes, I noticed at my very first introduction to him as I entered the room how terribly active he is."

"We are not making this up," said Davis. "It's true."

"You, Davis, at least have the good sense to appear sheepish about it. Who has keys to this laboratory?"

"I had them all changed. I have the only copies, here in my pocket. They are all the best-quality Yale locks. He has continued to be found in new positions on the floor, despite the fact that no one can possibly get into the lab."

Higg tapped the metal door with his stick. His good humor

was, for the moment, gone. He loved being in the field, but he did not like foolishness. Then he brightened. At least this was better than sitting at a desk in London. He enjoyed being with young people, even ones who had become confused about what was, and was not, possible.

"I am glad," he said, "that I decided to come up here to visit with you. We have much to discuss."

The meeting was held in the main Portakabin. It was a crowd, with the dozen and more of the team all in the place at the same time, but it had happened before, during a break, or on the rare occasions Peter had wanted to address them all. The last time they had all sat like this had been when Peter told them Langton was buying them all a pint.

Now Peter leaned against the wall, his eyes half closed as though in concentration. Dr. Higg was standing, with his winning smile, and lovable hound wrinkles. Peter was, indeed, concentrating, and he was listening to what Higg was saying. But what Higg said made Peter burn with a great inner glee, and Peter wanted to hide this.

Peter was delighted at the talk about the site being haunted. The rumors were of keenest interest to him. They fit his hopes exactly. He had not heard until now what apparently everyone else had been discussing. The Skeldergate Man was moving at night. Every night, for the past week, in a locked room.

The faces of the workers, and of Mandy and Jane, were strangely tense. Peter wanted to laugh. They believed this stupid rumor! They thought the man-shaped sack of leather was walking around at night.

Even Davis was worried. Peter had to cover his mouth to disguise a smile. Davis, the great archaeologist, the man who could steal women away from Peter without any effort at all, was afraid of an old puddle of skin. This was all, thought Peter, entirely wonderful.

Dr. Higg explained this rumor, and said it was best to talk about such matters, and not try to keep matters like this a secret. "At the end of the day," he said, "there are no secrets."

He went on to explain that when people worked with the dead it sometimes brought out troubling feelings. He had worked on the excavations of hundreds of graves in his career, and he himself had suffered the occasional nightmare. It was natural. The team members were human, and they had a natural respect for the dead, and that respect at times spilled over into something like fear. They should be rational, though, and understand the cause of their fears.

The team visibly relaxed as Dr. Higg spoke. This was exactly what they had all needed to hear. "Sometimes," Dr. Higg said, "a rumor has gotten around a camp that unexplainable things were happening. Tools moving around at night, finds trays emptying themselves out, skulls moving from shelf to shelf. We've all heard of this sort of thing, and some of these things have been, from what Mr. Langton has told me, happening here.

"Sometimes there is some basis for these rumors. Sometimes tools do move around. We don't know why. Sometimes a specimen simply will not stay in the drawer where we put it. We have no way of explaining such things. Things sometimes simply climb around a bit when we aren't looking."

The team chuckled over what had, earlier, seemed deadly sinister.

"As to why our friend Mr. Skeldergate keeps swimming off his table, I have no idea, but I assure you that I intend to look into it and discover what is taking place in the laboratory, and I shall report back to you. I want you to know one thing that is completely unquestionable. The dead do not move about, or trouble themselves with our poor living affairs. The dead are harmless, as much as we might wish them to be potent. They have no power, neither the evil dead, nor the beloved dead who we wish could come and visit us, no matter how frightening we might, in a way, find the thought. The dead do nothing. Only the living can act, and whatever moves the mattocks about, or causes accidents to take place, and whatever shifts the bog man about on his table, rest assured it is not a supernatural power. It is a physical power, one that a rational mind can entirely comprehend."

Peter agreed, of course, despite his glee at the rumors. There were no ghosts. Ghosts were for children, and for childish adults. The dig had certainly had no power over Peter in any way. He was entirely unchanged by any of the so-called supernatural events. Peter was, he thought, a rationalist. He did not even believe in God, much less in evil spirits, or whatever it was that frightened even such clear-headed people as Jane. Jane, the self-possessed beauty, was clearly concerned. He could tell by looking at her.

There had been, he would admit to himself, a return of that voice. That quiet, little boy's voice.

Those naughty, naughty creatures. How bad they were, and how well they would be punished for their naughtiness. He knew what cats were, and what they craved.

It had come back to him, that wonderful lust he had entirely forgotten. His nights were so precious to him now. Three more creatures had fallen to him, and the pleasure was such a sweet song that to even think of it here, in this warm room, was enough to make him hard.

What impressed Peter was that even such a solid man as Davis was at least somewhat taken in by the thought that the bog man was getting up off his table and shadowboxing at night. It was all very amusing.

It was more than amusing.

Peter had a plan.

15

"I'm glad you spoke to us all today," said Davis. "It helped."

"I had begun to wonder if the task here might be too troubling for you," said Dr. Higg.

"Not at all," Davis was quick to respond. "I like it here very much."

Higg nodded, observing the younger man, and enjoying what he saw. Davis was a sensitive man. Most intelligent men were, in one way or another. But Davis thrived on work. That was very important.

He had asked Davis and Langton to join him at the White Swan. He had, actually, asked Peter Chambers as well, but the man had explained that he was not feeling particularly well.

Higg sipped his whiskey. It was that furtive young man, with his lean face and darting eyes, who had him troubled.

"Something is bothering Peter," said Higg. "We all know— that is, the three of us here—that he has had some emotional troubles in the past. I wonder if the stress of all this has been too much."

"He's always been a quiet sort of man," said Davis. "He seems about the same as always to me."

Higg had his doubts, but perhaps Davis was right. It was difficult to understand a man like Peter Chambers.

Davis guessed that the two administrators would like to be alone together, so he stood and excused himself.

"No need to run off," said Dr. Higg.

Davis thanked him, and turned away.

"I was thinking I might drop by and visit the laboratory just briefly tonight," said Dr. Higg. "Actually, I wanted to spend a moment there alone. Do you have—?"

Davis gave him the keys, but pressed himself on Dr. Higg as an eager helper. "I'd be glad to show you anything you want to see in the lab."

Davis had been disturbed by the apparent movement of the Skeldergate Man, much more than he had even liked to admit to himself. Dr. Higg had seemed like a monument of rationality, and Davis was as grateful as a little boy that the distinguished scientist had paid them a visit. He had too much respect for Dr. Higg to argue with him. If he wanted the keys to the lab, he could have them.

"I want to putter about for a bit on my own, if I may," said Higg, cradling the keys in his hand. "You run along."

Davis did just that, shook hands with Dr. Higg and thanked him, and then left Higg with Langton's balding pate for company. Langton wasn't such a bad sort, but he was hardly a man of vigor and new ideas. Higg envied the young for their superstitions, and their need for reassurance. It took energy to be uneasy.

"It was, I must agree, a marvelous speech today," said Langton.

"Hardly that. Hardly a speech, and only a bit of common sense." Why was a compliment from Langton so irritating? "They are good, hardworking young people. That's what counts."

Music played, when it had been so comfortable and quiet. It was some displeasing thumping sort of music. It did not last long. When it was quiet again, Higg leaned toward Langton. "I am going to do some research tonight."

"Indeed." Langton blinked.

Higg nodded. "I am going to spend the night in the room with our friend."

"Peter?"

"Oh no, heavens no, dear Charles. You can be really amusing.

Please pay attention. I am going to spend the night with our friend the Skeldergate Man."

Langton smiled uneasily. Then, seeing that it was not a joke, he twitched. "Is that wise, do you think?"

"My dear Charles, do you suppose there is any danger whatsoever?"

"How could there be?"

"Precisely. There can be no danger, and I would like to find what sort of draft or tremor or prankster it is that moves our ancient friend from the table to the floor each night."

Langton grew solemn. "Do you really intend to spend the night there?"

"Alone, unless you intend to join me. I've spent worse nights in the field. I was bitten by a rattlesnake in New Mexico once on getting out of my sleeping bag. We were excavating pueblos near Taos. It was dark, and he had found my body warmth somehow pleasant. Fortunately, I was sleeping with my boots on, and the snake was so ill prepared he merely scratched the leather and left two little spurts of venom. He wasn't a very large snake, poor fellow. The men we had with us shot him and skinned him within a minute. He bit a dog when he was dead. The dog was very sick, but didn't die. The only time I can imagine a dead creature doing anything like harm. But here, you have me reminiscing, and this is very much unlike me."

"You should write your memoirs, William," said Langton. He was irritated with Dr. Higg. Langton felt vaguely responsible to Higg as long as he was in York. Higg would not have traveled to York if Langton had somehow managed to keep things sorted out. Langton was not nervous about the Skeldergate Man, but he was hardly going to sit up all night with Dr. Higg, who had twice his energy, and would no doubt want to spend the night discussing cranial volume or body art among the Papuans or some other ungodly subject. Langton admired Higg, but did not crave his constant companionship.

Besides, if you really considered it, there was something wrong about spending a night in that room. Langton couldn't decide what it was. Something willful and stubborn and something else, too. It seemed, at bottom, very unwise. Langton could not suppose why. Langton himself had a wife and a border collie, and it was late. The dog would want a walk, and it would be fortunate to make it to Clifton Green tonight. Langton was tired.

Langton asked after Higg's requirements. Bedding would not be necessary, said Dr. Higg. He would spend the night reading, and writing up his notes. It would, he said, be like the nights in the Yucatán, when rumors simmered that bandits were about and the unarmed scientists had to take turns staying up all night, reading to the hiss of a Coleman lantern.

Langton walked Higg to the college. Higg swung his blackthorn in one hand, and jingled the keys in the other. He would be glad to be alone. For some reason, he had spent too much time thinking about the past during the last day or two. And worse, talking about the past. Higg was far from young, but he was a man with many present interests. Nostalgia had no place in his intellectual landscape.

Langton wished him good night, and added, to Higg's mild annoyance, "Are you quite sure you want to do this, William?"

"Entirely, thank you, Charles."

At last, Higg was alone. He fumbled with the keys, and found the right one, door after door, until he stood in the brightly lit lab, thankful for his overcoat. He selected the one key he had not used, and strolled toward the room that held his friend, the Skeldergate Man.

Why did he feel that this was an adventure of sorts? He simply wanted to establish the fact that there was nothing at all supernatural about the Skeldergate Man, or the laboratory, and communicate it to his young colleagues. All it would take would be patience.

He could see his own breath. He unlocked the door, and the door handle would not open for a moment. It felt as though someone held it from the inside. Higg was not a particularly good man with devices of any sort. He supposed a door handle was, in its way, a device.

The door opened, as though relenting. Foolishly, Higg found himself hesitating before the darkness of the room within. For some reason, he had not expected dark. He wanted to laugh at himself. He had never in his life been, even for a moment, afraid of the dark.

He found the light switch. The fluorescent tubes stuttered and went out. They came on again, and stayed on, making that high, insect hum.

The Skeldergate Man was under a black plastic sheet. Its profile was discernible. It could be nothing else; only a human body would have had these contours. Higg found the only chair in the room, and pulled the results of the CAT scan from his inner pocket. He decided to leave his overcoat on in this cold room—cold and silent, except for the high, fine sound of the lights. He should have brought a flask of coffee.

Hadn't there always been that footstep just beyond hearing, that skull he could not bear to have sitting beside him as he slept? He had always put away a skull he might have sitting about before he switched out the lights. He had always had an imagination.

He unfurled a sheaf of paper showing what looked like the topography of a complicated range of mountains. He let the paper fall to the floor. He really, indeed, should have brought a flask of coffee, or something to read aside from this report on the smuggling of icons from the Soviet Union, and this one, on the wear patterns on molars from the Roman cemetery in Arles. Both subjects would have been fascinating at any other time, but now, for some reason, he could not concentrate on them at all.

It had, after all, been a long day, but he was accustomed to work. He was not tired. It was something else. He was not sleepy, not a bit—there was something entirely different troubling him and making it impossible to read. Or to sit still. Or to think of anything else.

Except for the figure under the black plastic sheet. He had known a young woman working on the excavations in the ancient crypt of Spitalfields who had gone quite mad from working with the dead. It had been an especially difficult task, with high lead levels in the air from the old coffins, and both "wet" dead and "dry" dead, as they called them. Higg did not blame the young woman for her troubles, but usually these mental problems were the result of a preexisting stress. The more morbid aspects of archaeology could be easily dissipated by a rational approach. Naturally, it was a very good idea to screen the younger scientists carefully, and in this light Peter still troubled him.

Higg was itching with a very great desire to peek under the plastic sheet. Just a peek.

Why shouldn't he, really, if one really stopped and thought about it? He could take a quick look, if he wanted to. Why was he even hesitating?

But he did hesitate. He should sit still, and read. There was no reason to pay any notice to the poor fragment of a human life that lay under the black plastic sheet.

Just a peek.

There had always been that sense that something was watching, on those star-filled nights in New Mexico. One of the old wranglers who handled the horses had laughed about the snake. "It is a gift," he had said. "Of luck from the other world."

From the Other World.

This was impossible. He was sitting, unable to read, fidgeting like a boy. The thing to do was very simple: stand up, and step over to the table and take that good, long peek, just to get it done and out of the way. Then he could sit and read, and the article about the icons was really quite interesting, in its way.

Don't.

Higg was extremely annoyed with himself now. His body would not rise from the chair. He could not reach the table from here. It was quite impossible for him to examine the Skeldergate Man without rising from the chair—as he did now, at last—and stepping to the table.

At last his arms and legs were cooperating. This was very kind of them, he thought. Now I will put my hands on the black plastic, and pull it to one side.

No.

His hand was trembling. This was most irritating, and made Higg think that perhaps there might be some medical trouble. There was no reason he could think of that would account for this extreme cold he was feeling, and the great difficulty he had in getting his hands to obey his will.

Higg calmed himself, taking deep, regular breaths, and realized as he did so that he had been, and probably still was, afraid. Afraid! It was really thoroughly absurd, and he knew one quick way to dispel any such nonsense immediately from his mind.

He grasped the edge of the plastic between his thumb and his forefinger, and he whisked the sheet aside.

16

Her reflection was sliced by the surface of the water. She was drifting toward him.

He began to walk toward her. The water broke under one foot, but then healed around it, and the other foot pressed the breathing water down, and the water supported his weight.

He began to try to cry out, and wrestle with the dream, but he could not speak, and he could not move. Margaret was continuing, wafting toward him, and he began to drift toward her. He wanted to break the dream, and he couldn't. They were approaching each other more and more quickly.

He held her. He could feel the shape of her body in his arms. Margaret, he wanted to say. After all these months. The change began, as it always did. The skin of her face wrinkled, a fan of fissures breaking across it. Flakes of flesh fluttered away, exposing the carbon-black skull.

"Davis," said a voice.

Who is it?

"Davis. Wake up."

Davis woke.

Irene held him.

"You were moaning so, Davis," she said. "Was it your nightmare again?"

He did not speak for a moment. "Yes. The nightmare. Did I try to get out of bed?"

"In your sleep?"

"Did I try to get up and walk?"

"You simply lay there asleep and moaning, and I woke you up. If you had begun to walk, I might not have awakened you, though. I have heard that it can be very frightening to be awakened while walking in sleep."

He was still shivering. He ran his hands through her hair. "What will you do," he said, "when I begin to walk in my sleep again?"

"I will walk with you."

Davis laughed, despite himself.

"I will go with you, and all will be well."

"I wonder if it will be that simple."

"Yes, Davis, I think so."

They both lay down again, and soon Irene was breathing slowly, lost in sleep.

Margaret.

She had always been unfaithful to him, from the very beginning. She had been quick to love him. "I want to stand like this forever," she had said in the rain of Quintana Roo, having turned to him suddenly. His arms had closed around her. That night she had told him she loved him, and would never want any other man but him, and this was surprising as well as exciting.

In the scrub jungle, with mosquitoes and iguanas, they began an affair. Davis believed that she had, in truth, loved him. Certainly, after a few days, he loved her. But there were so many other men, from the beginning. As soon as they reached San Diego, where Davis was lecturing that summer, she was on the telephone, hanging up when he entered the room. She broke lunch dates, calling him at the last minute, and there was that feeling about her of other men.

He had asked her to marry him, thinking that she would change. There was a quick taxi ride to the airport, and a short flight to Las Vegas, and then telephone calls to friends and family to explain, after the fact, what they had done. Everyone accepted the suddenness of it. The consensus seemed to be that they were the two smartest and best-looking people anywhere on the horizon, and that naturally they would rush to be married. It was the only rational thing to do.

But she insisted on going to conventions alone. Davis encouraged her, because he knew that she should continue her own career. When she returned she was passionate, but Davis knew. There was no pretending after a while. She had affairs. He challenged her and she shrugged. "You knew how I was. There are many attractive men in archaeology."

She drank. Often in the morning, before breakfast, she would have a vodka and beef bouillon she described as "medicine." Of course, she needed medicine, Davis knew, to help her through the hangover from the night before. But on the few occasions she would actually make it to a lunch in San Francisco, at one of their favorite North Beach spots, she would inhale prelunch martinis, and share a bottle of wine, and then have her dessert martini, or two. She showed little damage from all of this, except that she went to bed shortly after the seven o'clock news, and in the morning sometimes put ice cubes into a washcloth for the puffiness around her eyes.

She gave brilliant lectures, and wrote well, although her articles were not often published, being in various ways argumentative, challenging the articles that had appeared in a journal just months before. Editors "admired" her work, but tended to feel "this was not the right time." If one scientist reasoned that a jaw found in the Calico Mountains was that of an early Indian based on C-fourteen and location of the find, Margaret would write an article proving that the Calico Mountains were so acid that no bone would last ten thousand years, no matter what the carbon test indicated.

She loved parties, the kind of party that finds its place in the society pages, parties that required dresses as expensive as automobiles, and involved a pre-party drink at Donatello's and champagne and cocktails and after-party drinks, and sometimes Davis would not know where she was for days. Yet no one seemed to perceive that Davis and Margaret were not a loving, happy couple. Davis was always flying back from New York as Margaret was leaving for a party on a yacht in Tiburon, or flying to give a paper in Houston.

He had left her once, and rented an apartment in Sausalito. He had reasoned with her, and fought with her, but it had done no good. She begged him tearfully to come back to her, and he had.

He loved her, and her absences made him see her as, unavoidably, a fantasy figure as well as an actual woman. He was always planning that perfect weekend, in their own apartment beside San Francisco Bay, or in a cabin at Lake Tahoe, or on a spur-of-the-moment fling in Rome. These weekends never occurred. There were only fights, embraces, and passion, and afterward the cycle would begin again. If I could only win her completely, he thought.

Archaeologists who are also celebrities do not necessarily have strongboxes of Spanish gold. Margaret loved cars, and what she could not buy she leased, and, from time to time, borrowed. There was a series of accidents, often in a distant city. Davis knew he was losing her, but he could not guess to what.

But the source of his guilt, and the reason the dream kept returning, was in a meeting in a sunny coffee shop on Solano Avenue.

She had looked beautiful, and Davis saw how ironic it was to meet for lunch like this, like lovers who still did not know each other well. She had mentioned that perhaps they should discuss their future, as though seeing her over breakfast, or on her way out the door to a convention, did not give them a chance to talk about their lives. But she was right, of course. Their lives had become a string of brief meetings. They had to meet like this, like near strangers, to discover something resembling a future.

Davis was due to deliver a paper on early navigation in San Diego that weekend. He was awash in concepts of landfall and dead reckoning. It was a convention of archaeologists from around the world, and the chance to deliver a paper there was a genuine prize.

She had ordered espresso, and said she was not hungry, and after a moment Davis saw that her energetic glow was the aura of pure panic.

"Davis," she said, and she nearly could not speak. "I wake up in the morning, and I can't remember anything after Eyewitness News."

Davis had heard this before, but never with such feeling. "You should get help," he said. He added, with what he hoped sounded like sympathy, "I want to help you, Margaret."

"I'll change," she said, tugging a Kleenex from her purse. "You don't think I can, do you?"

"I think you can."

"But listen to how you say it. So tentatively. I'm off to Seattle tonight. Did you forget?"

"I knew you were going somewhere."

"Come with me. Please, Davis. We can—"

She saw him shake his head and look away.

Her voice was husky, like the voice of a much older person when she said, "It would mean so much to me."

"I have that paper to give. The one on ship's ballast and how Drake enjoyed his California vacation."

He had tried to make a joke of it, but Margaret bunched her Kleenex tightly. "You've been working on that paper for months."

She said this with a smile that troubled him.

If he tasted his coffee now, he knew it would taste like purest acid. "I'll fly back up to see you in Seattle. Right after I give my paper."

She did not speak for a while. Then, "I don't think I'll go. I can't stand to be alone anymore. It's just the University of Washington. I'll tell them I'm sick."

"They'll talk, you know."

"What will they say?"

"You know exactly what they'll say."

"They'll say that I drink. And I do. Can the truth really hurt me?"

He did not respond to that question, because Davis believed that of all things in the world, it is truth that is most relentless. "Then I'll fly back early. I'll just spend Friday night, just enough time to slaughter a few French vowels and try to dig up my German. I'll give my paper at ten, and be back in time for lunch."

But he should have canceled. He nearly did. It would have been so easy to make a phone call, and bow out of this convention. There would always be another. But the work he had put into the paper, and his vanity, and perhaps even his exasperation with her, made him feel that he would go for just the one night.

"You promise you'll fly back early?"

Davis promised. And he did fly back early, after giving the paper, a shimmering swimming pool in the distance behind a flock of scholarly heads.

There had been applause, and then offers to have lunch. Davis managed to excuse himself in three languages, and each time added, in English, that he had promised to see his wife for lunch, six hundred miles away.

It was his last morning as an ignorant man. The truth had not

100

broken upon him, and would not until he returned to phone calls from friends as soon as he had stepped into the empty apartment.

No one needed to accuse him. He knew the truth. Margaret had every right to resent him, to hate him, to hold him responsible for her death. He should have been with her.

At two o'clock that morning Margaret had driven a vintage MG the wrong way down the Bay Shore Freeway. He had imagined it so many times he felt that he had seen it happen. Cars avoided her, spinning and squealing. She drove, seemingly oblivious, past the Army Street turnoff. The night was wet. There was a drizzle, fine as flour. She collided with a Chrysler driven by a man wanted in two states for various crimes. To make his trip easier, this man had carried plastic antifreeze containers of gasoline in the back seat.

The two cars burned for three hours, and what was left was, judging from the single agonizing *Chronicle* photograph Davis had seen before he could avoid looking, a pile of white ash.

Maybe she hadn't felt it. Maybe she hadn't known.

Grief had devastated Davis. For weeks he had been unable to focus a single thought except *She's gone.*

He only gradually returned to his lectures, and the lab at the university campus. When the dreams, and the sleepwalking began, after three or four months, he had known he might never recover fully from losing Margaret.

Perhaps he never would. Only now, with Irene beside him, could he imagine a time when, like a normal person, like his old self, he would experience, day after day, a productive life. He was lucky to have called Dr. Higg. Dr. Higg had always believed in the power of work, and Davis had always believed in the magic of travel.

Irene was a wonder. For a moment Davis felt a feeling he could only call gratitude. Toward Dr. Higg. And toward Irene, and the powers, whatever they were, that knitted life.

Davis was up at dawn, and went for a quick run on the rugby field beside the Ouse. It felt cold, but there was no frost, and as the sun leaked over the Minster in the distance, its light was warm.

"Today we will go visit a very important man," said Irene. "We will visit a man who knows everything about the history of York. I have mentioned him to you many times. He is called August Foote. You have no doubt seen his bookstore."

Davis unlaced his Reeboks. "I need to spend as much time with Dr. Higg as possible today."

"But he returns to London at noon. You will have all afternoon."

"How can Mr. Foote help us? Or are we simply working on educating me on the rich lore of York? You don't have to convince me. I love this town."

"There are things you do not know."

Davis conceded that without a murmur. He knew very little, certainly, about life and death, and most of that was probably wrong.

"Except that Dr. Foote does not like archaeologists, so you will find it a very amusing meeting."

"He doesn't like what?"

"He hates us." Irene laughed. "You will be very amused."

"How could someone dislike archaeologists? Or is it our team in particular he doesn't like?"

"You will see. He will especially hate you when he sees you. I had to beg him. 'Oh, please, do talk to us.' He is a very grumpy man."

"I think I'll go back to London with Dr. Higg."

"It will be very amusing."

They had planned to meet at Langton's office, but Mrs. Webster, the secretary, was setting forth the cups and spoons unattended by Higg or Mr. Langton. She had not heard from either man, and she was irritated. "They could at least ring me and explain that they had a delay, couldn't they? It wouldn't be too much to ask, would it?"

Jane sat with her arms crossed, looking both prim and sullen. She wished Davis and Irene a good morning in a sweet voice, but did not meet anyone's eyes. Mandy was delighted to see everyone, it seemed, and described a Jimmy Stewart movie she had seen on television the night before as "his best movie, fullstop." Irene offered that she had not seen it, and Mandy began telling the plot.

Peter arrived, his work boots slashed with dew, looking disheveled, although this was usual for a field-working archaeologist. His fingers trembled as he rolled a cigarette. "I do hate meetings," he said. "Especially when they are so slow starting."

This one was remarkably slow starting. The entire tale of the Jimmy Stewart western was unwound by the time Davis suggested a telephone call to Mr. Langton.

Irene and Mandy chatted happily. Jane read articles, which she underlined with a nylon-tipped red pen. Peter smoked, and gazed at his cigarette smoke thoughtfully. Davis gathered that his old colleague did not feel up to conversation. Peter seemed determined to create the world's oddest-looking cigarette. Each one he rolled was more peculiar in shape than the one before it. Davis considered it a miracle of physics that smoke could be drawn through such paper tubes.

"Mr. Langton extends his most earnest apologies. He says," reported Mrs. Webster, "that he overslept."

She paused, and repositioned the coffee cups. "The alarm, he said."

"It didn't go off," said Mandy.

"It happens, doesn't it?" said Mrs. Webster.

When Langton arrived, pink-cheeked and wispy but otherwise much as he always looked, he gazed quickly around without managing to speak. He apologized, vaguely, but was evidently alarmed.

"Dr. Higg isn't here yet," Davis volunteered.

Langton blinked. "I don't like this at all," he said.

Davis and Mandy asked a stream of questions, but Langton hurried to his desk and dialed one number, and then another.

"I don't like it a bit," he said, replacing the receiver. "No answer at the laboratory. I don't know what to think."

Davis asked a series of questions which Langton ignored, until at last he answered all of them in a burst. Dr. Higg had gone off to spend the night in the laboratory. Langton was not sure why, but it was no doubt to discover how the Skeldergate Man was moved during the night. "Or some such thing, I don't know. He's a very determined man, you know."

Davis turned to Peter. "Did you bring your car?" he asked.

"Not today," said Peter, tapping ash from his cigarette. "I walked."

Davis excused himself, and ran down the stairs, into the bright, cold morning. It was an easy run up Gillygate. The only pedestrians were people in a hurry to get somewhere, and there were no window-shoppers or tourists.

Davis ran up Lord Mayor's Walk, and sprinted across the street in the heavy traffic. At first he had been only moderately worried. This was only a precaution, to make sure that Dr. Higg was not, for

103

example, trapped in the lab by a door that stuck, or some equally silly accident.

But as he bounded across the glistening green grass, sending a blackbird from its place on the garden wall, he was not so sure. He reasoned with himself that by acting so hastily he was causing himself to worry for no real reason.

The outside door to the lab was unlocked. Davis could not decide whether this was a good sign or not. It meant, he decided, thumping down the dark stairs, that Higg had not left the lab. He surely would have remembered to lock the door.

Unless he had been in a great hurry.

The stairs seemed endless, but each door was unlocked until he stood in the great lab itself, brightly lit and cold, as always.

Everything was exactly as it should be, thought Davis. Every table was straight. The finds trays were all stacked neatly. Everything was in perfect order.

Davis approached the door to the small room at the end very slowly. He called out Dr. Higg's name several times, but there was no sound. The door to the small room was just slightly ajar. This was a good sign, thought Davis.

But it wasn't really. All it meant was that no one had shut the door behind them. And it showed that the light was still on in the small room.

Davis did not want to move.

Hurry. There might be something wrong. Be quick.

Davis warily crept to the door and parted his lips to say Dr. Higg's name, but he did not bother. He put his forefinger on the door handle and pushed.

The door would not open. Davis put his weight against it. The door reluctantly lurched open, slowly and more slowly, with a weight behind it the nature of which Davis guessed, with a knot in his stomach.

Dr. Higg was on the floor, bent sideways where the door had half pushed and half rolled him. His face was a mask of horror—mouth agape, eyes wide. There was a sigh from Dr. Higg as Davis rolled him flat, and warm breath came and went at his nostrils, although his eyes continued to stare.

Only then did Davis register in his mind what he had seen as he squeezed into the room, in his haste to attend to Dr. Higg.

Davis stood slowly, straightening to his full height.

The Skeldergate Man was gone.

104

17

Dr. Higg nearly died as the stretcher was trundled from the ambulance into the corridor. Davis was trotting alongside the unconscious scientist and the ambulance crew when Dr. Higg went gray, and his head fell to one side.

His eyes stared, but slowly rolled up into his head. His tongue was blue.

The corridors swallowed Dr. Higg, and Davis paced until Irene and the rest of the team arrived. Langton moaned and paced, sat and just as quickly stood again.

Davis put out a hand to comfort the distraught Langton, but the poor man stared distractedly. "What will it be next?" he murmured.

"Surely," said Jane, "they'll be able to help him here."

Langton, however, turned away. "A disaster," he moaned. "Unmitigated disaster."

A nurse with a hat like a white dove took Davis aside and wrote neatly on a form as Davis answered her questions. He could not tell her about the missing Man, however. He had taken a few seconds to stammer that bit of news to Irene and Langton over the telephone. That news had stunned even Irene.

"He was lying unconscious on the floor?" asked the nurse. She did not seem to believe Davis.

Not exactly unconscious, Davis wanted to say. An unconscious man does not wear a look of horror.

He tried to ignore her question.

"Was there any sign of an accident?" asked the nurse, with a show of patience.

Not exactly, unless you can call whatever he had seen an accident. Davis attempted an explanation. "It was as though he had seen something that frightened him."

"What might that have been?"

Good question, he told himself. What did Dr. Higg see in the room at midnight? Go ahead and tell her what you really think. Go on. She won't believe you, anyway. Davis gave her what he hoped was a sincere smile. "I don't know."

The nurse dismissed him, plainly dissatisfied.

It was a long morning. At last a slim doctor with a freckled face stepped into the waiting room. He motioned to Davis, seeming to believe that Davis was the man in charge. Irene followed.

"How is he?"

"Very much alive, if that's what you mean," said the doctor, responding to Davis's question. The doctor wore a baggy shirt and a blue tie and introduced himself as Dr. Hall. He had a pleasant face, but questioning eyes. "Alive, I would say, but hardly well. He's quite ill, and I think he still may not recover."

Davis could not breathe.

"He may die," the doctor added. "Of a very unusual cause."

He led Davis and Irene to Dr. Higg's bedside.

Dr. Higg's eyes were closed, and his breathing seemed slow—too slow, like a man who had been pulled from icy water. His lips were still gray-blue. Dr. Hall nodded as if to say: You see what I mean.

Leading them from the room he continued, "Can you tell me what happened?"

"I wish I knew," said Davis. Langton had insisted that the theft of the Skeldergate Man be kept secret. The press was to hear nothing. The Skeldergate Man was very popular, and had stimulated the public to donate money. Davis had suggested that publicizing the

106

crime might make it easier to catch the criminals, but Langton was firm. "It might be simple hooligans," he said, "or it might be international thieves. We don't know, and we shouldn't discuss this with anyone."

But that wasn't the only reason the matter would be impossible to discuss, Davis realized as he walked down the corridor. How could he explain that possibly, just possibly, if you let your imagination run for a moment, Dr. Higg had seen something more terrifying than a thief?

Something much more terrifying.

It would earn the doctor's disbelief, and it would also be the sort of story impossible to keep out of the *Sun* and the *Star*.

"We think he must have interrupted a crime in the lab," said Davis at last. "A few things were missing."

Dr. Hall turned to face him. "Stolen?"

"Apparently."

"There's something very unsatisfactory about all of this. This man has suffered a profound shock. I have never seen anything like it before. I would like to know what, exactly, the nature of the shock was."

"So would I," said Davis, glad that he did not have to lie. "I would very much like to know what Dr. Higg saw. But I don't."

"I wish you would think about it," said Dr. Hall. "This man has nearly died of fright."

Outside, Davis was grateful for the chill. It told him that he was outside, under the sky, and not dying in a hospital bed.

"You will not want to go to see Mr. Foote now," said Irene. "You will find him too unpleasant."

Davis gazed about him, feeling dazed and disconnected from reality. The loss of the Skeldergate Man was a disaster in itself, and to see Dr. Higg so stricken made Davis feel that the world was a terrible place. "I'd welcome anything that took my mind off poor Dr. Higg."

"What do you suppose he saw?" said Irene.

"That's the sort of question I find too hard to answer. What do you think he saw?"

"Do you suppose," she asked impishly, "he saw the Skeldergate Man dancing around the room?"

"Waltzing. Waltzing around the room."

"Do you really think that, Davis?"

He shrugged. He didn't know what to think. "The thought occurs."

"Do things like that happen, Davis?"

"You sound as though you know they do."

Irene laughed sadly.

"You're trying to goad me into saying something foolish," said Davis. "Things like that don't happen."

He repeated it to himself over and over as they walked: Don't happen.

Foote's Book Shop was on High Petergate, nearly in the shadow of the Minster. The door invited them to ring the bell, but the button, when pushed, made no sound that Davis could hear. Irene touched the door, and it opened.

Davis was reluctant to open any doors that seemed at all mysterious. "Are you sure this is all right?"

"I visit this store very often. I buy books."

The stairs were narrow and steep. At the various landings books were piled, some looking entirely new, and some looking ancient. The carpet on the stair muffled their steps. As they climbed, out the small ripple-glassed windows they could glimpse the gables of the building across the street, and, looming above that, the Minster itself.

Irene paused outside a thick oak door. "You should wait out here, Davis," she said. "I will go in and I will announce you."

He could barely hear her voice from the next room. She seemed to be talking to total silence. She laughed, once, and then there was more silence. It was hot here on the stairs. He loosened his muffler.

Irene peeked out. "You may come in, Davis."

More books. They were arranged neatly, and had none of the dank, mildew smell that Davis associated with some old books. The room was warm, and the carpet a thick gray plush, quite new. The books addressed the general subject of sailing. There were books on clipper ships, and sailmaking, and navigation among the Fiji Islanders. Davis had time to discover a book or two, because Mr. Foote could not be seen.

"You should sit, Davis, in this chair. I will sit here. Be quick."

"We should wait until we're invited, don't you think?"

"Don't be silly."

108

Davis sat. He became aware that a tiny television camera was studying him from a nook. Davis swore quietly to himself. This was not what he needed. The world was disintegrating around him, and he was visiting the Great Recluse of York.

Irene smiled at him, and Davis was immediately cheered. This was as good a place to be as any he could think of. Besides, there were many questions to ask, and just possibly their invisible host was the man to answer them.

A door whispered, and a slim man with a bald head slipped into the room, shook Davis's hand, and found a perch on a stool, so quickly and quietly Davis could not speak for a moment.

"I appreciate the chance to meet you and—" Davis began, but Mr. Foote dashed his words aside with a gesture of contempt. No preliminaries, he seemed to say. No empty courtesy. It bores me.

"Tell me about Skeldergate," said Davis.

Mr. Foote sniffed.

Davis clasped his hands. He would be patient.

Mr. Foote worked a forefinger into his ear, and extracted it, examining the gleam of wax on his nail. "You want to know about that one particular site which your opportunistic profession has decided to rape." He smiled, quickly, brightly, and then the smile was gone, and his face blank.

"In a manner of speaking," said Davis, feeling slow of speech and gesture, dull, American in the most clumsy way. "Tell me, though, why you dislike archaeologists."

"It's a prejudice really, and I don't want to be unfair to you."

"I'm interested."

He was more than interested. He was beginning to feel the first light of anger. A great archaeologist lay near death as they spoke.

"You embarrass me. Irene's been telling tales. I feel, if you will forgive my being blunt, that archaeologists, like doctors and like lawyers, strive to appear harmless, but in fact they love the lurid find, the ancient battlefield, the hoard of treasure, and they love to see their faces in the newspaper."

Davis felt his anger die. "You accuse us of being human."

"And now that I hear myself being so terribly opinionated, I feel ashamed of myself. You want to know the secrets of Skeldergate." He was a much younger man than he had at first appeared. His quirky manner was, Davis thought, the result of youthful arrogance, and not fossilized ego.

Mr. Foote went on. "I could make a good deal of money in your field, or by writing books. I am an expert on haunted places. As to your haunted place: it's always been considered a place of haunting. Before the nineteenth-century warehouses there was a timber mill, and before that in the Elizabethan days, there was, as you know, a slaughterhouse. You will have found bones, horns, that sort of thing. Before that the area was given over to wool merchants, and before that a cooper and other such craftsmen lived and worked there, but all this you know from the work you have done.

"Before all of that, at about the time of the Norse incursions, about the ninth century, something happened there. Something very bad, because the early tax rolls of the sheriff here in York refer to a 'mordor pyt,' a murder pit, somewhere on this street. It was given as the reason so many men and women were hurt in peculiar accidents there. Priests were consulted, but the place is referred to more than once as a *platea nigromantiae,* vulgar Latin for 'place of necromancy,' which is, as you know, a way of telling the future through communion with the dead. No other place in York has such a reputation. We have the odd ghost, but nothing like that.

"So what might have happened there? Perhaps nothing. It might be all purest superstition, and without even the most modest basis in fact. But I believe that you have there a very important corpse, a man whose death was well remembered by everyone in the neighborhood. Why was such an important body dumped there, and left to become a scientific curiosity? I don't know. But I do have some further thoughts on who your Skeldergate Man might be. Do you care to go for a bit of a walk?"

Davis agreed heartily. He found himself enjoying this strange, thin man.

The three of them walked across Deangate, and passed before the great doors of the Minster. The wind was icy crossing the Minster green. They entered the Minster Library, and Mr. Foote greeted the men and women there with a wave or a nod, apparently preferring to speak as little as possible.

He whispered to a broad-shouldered, bearded man, and the three of them were let into a long, narrow room. The ancient floorboards were slick with wear, and groaned underfoot.

"There are many secrets here. This is York's equivalent to the secret manuscripts of the Vatican. Our arcana, our scandals, our mysteries are kept here—or, at least, the more ancient ones."

Mr. Foote climbed a ladder and made a "hmmm" of impatience. He climbed down, and rolled the ladder to a new place. "Ah." He dragged a large leather tome from a shelf. He gasped and nearly dropped it, and Davis helped.

They found a lectern, and Mr. Foote opened the book very carefully. "This is an eighteenth-century binding of a set of manuscripts collated in the fourteenth century. The texts themselves are very much older. You see the vellum and the gilt on some of the illuminated pages. Oddments, really, not belonging together. Ah, here is the page I want."

It was a golden brown chart of vellum so coarse it was very much a cured hide. The writing on it was so dim that at first glance the page seemed merely foxed. Looking more closely, Davis made out writing. "Northumbrian script," said Davis. "A cross between uncial and cursive. And something of a scrawl, too. This isn't very good penmanship."

"Can you read what it says here?" asked Mr. Foote, challengingly.

Davis read, translating from the Northumbrian Anglo-Saxon. "'In this year Lord Sigan became king, reigned for three months, and was himself killed by his son, Alfwold, who tried to secrete the body to disguise his crime. Alfwold secured the throne after bloody fighting.' (This is an unusual construction—*blood fechten*. I think our scribe might have been German.) 'King Sigan's body was never discovered, and the Norsemen marched upon us before God's justice could be done.'"

Davis stared at the words before him.

King Sigan's body.

"An unavenged death," said Mr. Foote. "An attack from the east by Vikings before the crime could be brought to justice. Alfwold, quite possibly, killed in the subsequent warfare, but the murder itself, an unholy regicide, never resolved."

"Spirits do not like to be unavenged, Davis," said Irene. "Or at least, we think they do not."

The ancient script seemed to fade back into the page as Davis gazed at it. It had always been weak ink, perhaps made of bark. It would have been like writing with weak tea. This script had been scratched onto the page during a time of hardship. There would come a time when this writing would fade completely, and become invisible.

111

Mr. Foote, as though reading Davis's thoughts, closed the book.

"You have disappointed me, Mr. Foote," said Irene. "I have told Davis how very grumpy you have always been, and you have been so very friendly."

"Tell me, do you believe in ghosts, Mr. Lowry?" said Foote, climbing the ladder.

Davis did not answer. He did not believe in ghosts, but it seemed to him that what one believed or did not believe did not matter.

"Nor do I. Do you believe in poltergeists? A phenomenon in which objects seem to have a life of their own. Move about, break, explode." The volume slipped back into its place on the shelf. Mr. Foote looked down at them. "As though spirits inhabited them."

"Davis does not believe in spirits," said Irene. "He is a rational man."

Mr. Foote leaped lightly from the ladder. "I said 'as though.' I don't believe in spirits, either. But I do believe that what you have at your dig, among all your microscopes and finds trays, permeating all the artifacts you discover there, is a poltergeist."

Mr. Foote paused, and brushed his hands together.

"And if it can compel objects," said Mr. Foote, "it can compel anything. Perhaps even people."

Or, thought Davis, cause a man to die of fright.

18

This was a strong one, bigger than all the others, and Peter had watched him for several nights.

It was dark and there was a cold wind. Spits of wind struck his face as he carried the box along the Ouse, avoiding the quaking puddles of rainwater. There were stars, but they came and went as clouds sliced the sky. A lash of rain made him blink.

He had his special gloves with him, the stout leather gloves he had bought at the gardening and home repair store near Fishergate. If only the chorus of sounds in his head would be quiet for a moment. If only he could stop and consider.

But he could not stop. It was pleasure, wasn't it? And it rid the world of these nasty beasts, didn't it? Because they were nasty, there was no question about that.

Only this time he found himself weeping as he laughed. It was wrenching, this confusion. He knew he was doing the right thing, and he knew he would not stop.

But there was something wrong with him. It was just like all those years before. There had been something wrong then, too. He hated himself for his weakness. Why was he trembling so tonight?

He was disgusted with himself. He had a right to pleasure, just like any other man. Besides, this cat had a chance, not like the others, who had been weak. This cat was a fighter, much heavier than the others, a brawny male who was in excellent condition, a great gray stud of a cat.

This would be a battle. He relished this, and to be far, where no one would be able to hear, and to forestall what he knew would be sweetest pleasure, he carried the box to Clifton Ing, the vast black meadow.

It was wet here, and sometimes his feet sank into the turf. The cat was wheeling within the box, clawing, hissing. And howling— great savage howls that meant that the world would suffer for what was happening.

A battle. This would be sweet.

Then the cat was out. Peter had been nearly ready to stop, but it surprised him, and he grabbed for the cat, and missed. His left hand snatched and caught a hind leg, but this hand was not wearing a glove.

Fortunately, the cat did not think of fighting yet, only of escape. It clawed the air, and clawed the darkened grass, hissing and spitting, and screaming like a woman.

Then it thought of fighting.

It was on Peter's arm, and up his arm, to his face. Peter thrust the leather glove to protect his eyes, and the savage rear feet clawed the glove, tearing even that tough hide.

Peter ducked, but the beast was much heavier, and much stronger, than Peter had foreseen. The brute spat, lashing with its paws, and one claw tangled itself in Peter's hair. Peter cried out. He lifted the beast high into the air with his gloved hand, and could barely keep it there. The animal twisted, and jackknifed.

The cat was nearly off, vanished into the dark.

Only the many nights of cat hunting allowed Peter to react by reflex, without a chance to realize what he was doing. He had the cat's tail, before he knew what he had done, and the cat didn't understand what was happening, either. Otherwise the beast would not have wasted its time raking the wet grass, and the demon would have doubled up and buried its fangs into Peter. He tried too late, snapping and tearing at the air.

Peter swung the beast around and around by its tail. The animal screamed, and fought, and tried to double back to the fist that held it, but Peter swung hard. Twice the cat succeeded in seizing the hand, but Peter slammed the savage thing to the turf, and the cat lost its grip.

Peter's blood was streaming. It tickled as it ran down his wheeling arm. He had his gloved hand ready, and caught the cat's skull in the best grip he had ever used on a cat, and the cat wasted its effort on the air, and on the thick coat sleeve. The powerful hind legs tore the coat, but could not find his flesh. Peter was ready, approaching the keenest pleasure.

And past it, panting.

The cat kicked convulsively. He flung it aside, and it did not move again. He fell to his knees, and gazed at the black around him. It began to rain again, hurried, lancing drops.

He knelt, empty inside. Retching, and trembling.

19

"These people are the lowest of the low, aren't they?" The policeman was tall, and wore a black radio clipped to the lapel of his overcoat. "Thieves of one sort or another, the smart ones, the daft ones, all of them. The lowest of the low."

Davis hardly felt like arguing with a policeman. He reflected, looking out the window at the trenches, that archaeology usually did not involve much contact with the police. Davis did not know how "low" most thieves were. Perhaps some were not so low. Davis had very little experience with thieves.

"Although," said the policeman, "it looks as though you've got a clever one in this case. Someone low and clever, a real snake, whoever this one is."

"You have no leads as to where the—I hate to call him simply a body—where the Skeldergate Man might be?"

The policeman made a kind smile. "It's entirely too early for anything so concrete as that."

Davis reflected. "Sometimes when a bog man is found, people come forth and try to confess to its murder. I can think of several instances in which men came forth claiming that an ancient body was the wife they had killed years before. Sometimes two or three men come forth to claim the murder of a given body. Some murders have been solved in that way."

"The conscience does eat at a killer," said the policeman, perhaps not quite following what Davis was beginning to suggest.

"Is it possible that someone believes this is someone they killed? Maybe they stole the body to destroy it. Burn the evidence, in a way."

"This is an intelligent sort of a theory," said the policeman, plainly not willing to trade theories with a scientist. "We'll see what we can see."

When the policeman was gone, Davis got up and found himself a helmet. He was sick of things he could not understand. The policeman had told him something very disturbing, and he wanted to dig for a while. Since the Man had vanished, it was a waste of time to spend his days in the lab, especially now. He had been spending more and more time here at the dig. He badly missed working with Irene, but he felt his presence here was, somehow, good for morale. He found a square-bladed Bulldog spade in the jumble of tools in the shed.

It was true, he nearly laughed. Ridiculous. Nothing stayed where you put it here at the dig. If there was a poltergeist, perhaps it had a sense of humor.

A yellow Nally backhoe clawed earth, clearing a new trench. Peter scraped earth at the bottom of Trench Five, the pit that had nearly taken lives. No one else would climb into it. The work in all the trenches had slowed, with men working and then stopping to talk. Every worker was thoughtful, measuring, chipping away at the soil, but not seeming to make any progress. Davis sensed that the team counted on him, now, to make sense of everything. Peter had become thin and pale, and Mr. Langton seemed to spend most of his time sitting in his office, beside a telephone he hoped would not ring.

Dr. Higg continued to lie in what was essentially a coma, although Dr. Hall likened it to a trance. Dr. Hall had become slightly more friendly over the last several days. Perhaps he had seen Davis visiting his unconscious mentor so many times that he felt a degree of compassion. "It's a deep sleep, basically, from which he seems unable to awaken," Dr. Hall had volunteered one afternoon. "He's as close to dying as you can be without actually slipping over the threshold."

The wage-earning workers, like Skip and Oliver, had long ago decided that the site was haunted, and were accustomed to it. They worked more slowly now, Skip with his pneumatic drill blasting like warfare at one edge of the dig, Oliver plying his mattock in one trench. They moved cautiously, as though nothing could be trusted.
Unable to awaken. Davis stabbed the spade into a wall of earth. He did not not like that phrase, and it repeated itself tirelessly in his mind.

He emptied earth into a black bucket. Irene was working steadily on the finds trays in the lab. Davis was working steadily at keeping up appearances. This was hardly a group of archaeologists anymore. It was a group of frightened people. Even Mandy had become quiet, screening the piles of earth for the odd bit of antler or teeth.

"What did the police have to say?" It was Jane, blond hair cascading from under her helmet.

"Nothing at all conclusive," said Davis.

"You can tell me, Davis. I won't spread any secrets."

Jane, who had begun by being so flirtatious, had quickly seemed aloof. Davis leaned on his spade. He had seen daffodils, as yet unflowering, on the embankments of the city walls. A mild winter, Davis thought, and he knew that he was stalling in the crudest way, wanting to discuss the weather before he discussed what the police had said.

"The police know nothing," he said.

"They spoke to you for twenty-five minutes and had nothing to say?"

"Being police, they spent more time asking questions than answering them."

"You are, quite obviously, keeping some sort of secret."

Davis attempted a reassuring smile. "What I know makes no sense. I'm confused by what the police told me. Why should you be confused, too?"

"They've discovered something."

"Nothing very helpful." He would, in truth, be happy to share what he had heard.

"I believe I will stay here beside you until you tell me what it is."

She said it as though lightly, but Davis did not take Jane lightly. She was a determined woman.

118

"It's my fault," Davis began. "The police took prints in the room. Sprinkled powder, and used those little brushes. It took me days to clean up some of the smudges they left. Those powders can be very sticky." He took a scoop of syrupy mud, and dumped it into a bucket. "They got a pretty good palm print off the door handle. Ran it through their computer, or whatever they do. Didn't come up with anything. They were a little surprised. Usually they get a few possible matches, at least. This one wasn't even close."

"Certainly that wasn't their news."

Davis leaned on his spade again. He could not meet her bright, critical eyes. "Being a complete fool, I suggested that they try to match the palm print with someone we all know and love."

Jane did not speak.

"The Man himself, Mr. Skeldergate. We had prints made of his hands and feet about the time we did the body cavity blood test. And it came back a winner. The print belongs to a man who died one thousand two hundred years ago."

Davis shoveled mud for a moment. Then he stopped, and turned to Jane. "It could mean that the bog man got up and walked away. I believe it means that someone wants to make us think that he did, as a sort of joke."

Jane still did not speak.

"It is funny, I suppose," Davis mused, "in a cruel, ugly, putrid sort of way."

"I have been doing a good deal of thinking, Davis. Regarding my career. I haven't had the opportunity to really get to know you," she said briskly, "and this is something I will have to consider a misfortune. I believe that it would be better for me to resign from the Skeldergate dig. I understand that there is an exciting dig about to begin in London. Bits of the Roman wall, even an interval tower. It would really be so much better for my career to be associated with that—"

"Instead of this chain of lurid mishaps."

"Not the way I would put it. But, yes, actually."

When he was alone again, Davis squared off the corner of the trench. Alf grinned down at him, his arms writhing with tattoos. "Getting our hands dirty again today, are we? Can get to be a habit, that." He winched up the buckets one by one and trundled off with the wheelbarrow.

Davis heard the explosion after it knocked him down.

119

A flash, and a great slam, like a gigantic pane of glass blown in an instant. He had no memory of falling. He was sprawling, and then he was up again, pulling himself up the ladder.

The site was a photograph. No one moved. Pale faces were turned in one direction, toward a place behind one of the Portakabins. Davis himself felt unable to drag his body over the top of the ladder. The air was heavy, like wet sand.

Then, the scream.

Peter and Davis arrived at the back of the building at the same time, but both men staggered, half falling as another, smaller explosion flung a belt through the air. Engine parts hummed through the air past Davis's ear, and he crouched to make himself a smaller target.

The generator had blown up. It lay sideways on the ground, only half of it left, the rest of it demolished, littering the ground like bits of black gravel. Blue smoke welled upward from twisting red flames. Peter vanished for a moment, and then shielded his eyes and wrestled with a fire extinguisher.

Smoke swelled. It was blacker, now, and heavy, with a foul, metallic taste. Then Davis saw it.

It can't be true, he thought.

But the screams would not stop. He saw, and he could not pretend otherwise, although his mind cringed as Davis dived into the smoke and dragged Alf from the surging smoke.

Alf's words were impossible to make out, but Davis did not have to understand what he was saying. Alf gripped the stump of his handless arm. Scarlet spouts of red arced through the air.

They were a team again. Skip and Oliver arrived with bright red fire extinguishers, and Jane whipped a tourniquet around Alf's arm. The man was bellowing, and Davis was not certain it was pain, yet, so much as horror.

Smoke choked on the streams from the fire extinguishers. At times the smoke flashed away completely, only to fight back again from the charred, scattered machine.

There on the metal-strewn earth was a white star. Davis held his breath against the smoke, and dashed to the pale, flung treasure. It was still warm, and strangely bloodless in appearance. He carried it like a fragile treasure.

"His hand," Davis said unnecessarily. Everyone glanced away, and went sweaty pale. The cut had been clean, straight, surgeon-perfect. The hand had, now that he carried it well away from the smoke, a surprising amount of weight to it, real heft, as though a body were still attached to it, pressing downward.

Davis gritted his teeth, and wrapped the hand in a sheet of plastic. Just before he covered it he saw the head of a tattooed snake on the ball of the thumb, where it had lost the rest of its body.

The team was stunned, and had trouble speaking, but they did not lose their sense that Alf would survive. They encouraged him, prompted him to sit up, and when the ambulance arrived, they helped strap him into the stretcher. Alf was screaming less. His voice was torn to a thread of anguish, and he gasped, from time to time, for air.

The severed hand was wrapped in white plastic, and rested beside Alf like a second victim.

When the ambulance was gone, with its dancing blue lights, Peter stayed on his knees. Firemen arrived to soak the machine with water, but they spent as much time recoiling their hoses as they had dousing the smoke. The fire had been extinguished before they arrived.

The firemen departed. Spectators, hands in their coat pockets, watched from the distant gate, but they gradually melted away.

Peter stayed, sitting on the ground, alone. Davis found him there and asked how he was.

"There was no reason for it to do that," said Peter finally.

It was the first sentence Peter had spoken to Davis for days.

They both sat, gazing at the wreckage. A breath of smoke escaped a coil of ruined cowling. The area around the wrecked machine was black water.

"No reason at all," Peter continued.

Davis dreaded the words. "A mechanical failure," he suggested.

"What sort of mechanical failure would do that, Davis?"

"I have no idea."

"Generators don't blow up like that."

"Come on inside, Peter. Don't stay here like this."

Peter was trembling. Davis dragged him to his feet, and led him into the main cabin, to his desk. Peter sat with his head in his hands and could not stop shivering. Davis knew exactly how he felt. Davis offered Peter some tea, or some coffee, but Peter seemed not to hear.

It seemed to Davis that he could still feel the weight of the severed hand in his.

"I can see now what the trouble is," said Peter at last.

"Too many accidents."

"This was not an accident."

"Sabotage," Davis suggested. "Some twisted scientist somewhere envies us our success. He decides to make it difficult for us."

"Someone like me," said Peter with a sneer.

"I didn't mean anyone at all like you."

"Someone bitter. And smart enough to do this sort of damage."

"I had never considered you."

"You should have. But I swear this, Davis. I didn't make the generator explode. I wouldn't know how to do that if I wanted to. Poor Alf. I wouldn't want to do that to anybody."

Peter despised the sound of his own voice. The shock of the explosion was leading him to near confession. He was being very foolish. He should stop chattering like this. He scattered tobacco onto the floor when he rolled a cigarette. Sit still and be quiet, he commanded himself. The explosion has you a little bit shaken. That's quite understandable. No need to say anymore about it. He had been very good about working with Davis as though they were both nothing more than fellow professionals. It was essential to keep up the pretense, if only as a mental discipline.

"You hurt yourself," said Davis.

Peter pulled his sleeve down over a red scratch on his wrist. "It's nothing," he said hoarsely.

Peter hurried along the river, nearly running by the time he reached the stairs to his flat. It's best not to seem nervous, he warned himself. It's best to seem calm, to smile and return the greetings offered by people as they pass.

But he had to hurry. It was important to be sure that no one had entered the flat while he was gone. It was always possible that one of the cleaning girls might want to Hoover, and might for some reason fumble about in the closet.

Besides, things were not going entirely well. Well enough, but not entirely. He paced the sitting room, until he forced himself into a chair. Someone might hear him pacing. He must seem calm.

He stared at the closet door.

First of all, too many things were happening which had nothing to do with his plans. He had discovered Dr. Higg unconscious on the floor. That had been a rude shock. And the Skeldergate Man had been lying beside Dr. Higg, inexplicably. It almost made one believe in all this talk of spirits. Almost. But not quite.

And this explosion today. That made no sense at all. And then there had been a disappointment. Peter had built a structure for the bog man's body, a metal frame that allowed him to stand upright. He stood upright now, unseen, in the closet. That part worked admirably. There had, however, been a failure. Peter had hoped to design a mechanism that would cause the leather man to walk, and all of his notes and all of his genius—he could use the word privately, to himself—amounted to nothing.

All of his knowledge of radio-controlled devices could not supply him with a way to make the dead walk. It was as simple as that. He could mount the dead man on wheels, and have him move in that silly manner, but he would resemble a disturbing skateboarder more than anything else. And what Peter required was a means to drive Davis to the point of deathly fear.

Peter struck a Swan Vesta. Tobacco made him lucid, and he would need all of his mental acuity tonight. Because tonight he was going to experiment. He would not try to get the poor tanned gentleman to move. That was an old plan, to be set aside as colorful but unworkable.

Tonight, he would need to begin a new plan. He would experiment. And like any man about to experiment with something unheard of, he was perhaps a bit too excited.

He stood and stepped, as though afraid to wake someone, toward the closet. He had cut up an old black leather jacket. He had soaked old burlap he had bought at a jumble sale in motor oil. He had worked during the all too short nights, the nights that fled so quickly because he burned them up with his plans.

Convincing. He would need to look convincing. He opened the closet. The Man himself stood, covered with black plastic. The shapeless black rags, looking like a skinned man, hung on a hook.

The leather had been soaked in beef blood from the butcher's on Bridge Street. He had then pounded it epidermal-thin. The eyeholes fit exactly over Peter's own eyes. The black, supple skin was, as he slipped it on, now his own.

He felt it around him, this new skin, this second body. He was no longer Peter Chambers.

He had crafty fingers, he had to admit to himself. Skilled fingers, and a faith that there was always a way around any problem.

The tunic fit over him, and tied with thongs that looked age-clotted. He had considered actually wearing the Skeldergate Man's clothing, but this was a better fit. He had even considered wearing the Man's actual leathered skin, but there were enough stalactites of skull and femur within the skin to make this impossible.

Peter pulled the black skin tight around his face, and tucked the lips he had worked at so patiently over his own. How, he asked himself, will this ancient murder victim walk? Will he drag one foot? Will he stride slowly? Very slowly. As though he knew exactly where he was going.

He was conjuring the dead, and as he stood before the bathroom mirror he saw not Peter, the man who understood the ways of cat and man. He saw the dead, with a dead man's glittering eyes.

He laughed, dancing a strange jig into the kitchen. It was going to work! Tonight he would go for a ramble. Just a little stroll. Let the people of York continue to talk about spirits and a haunted site.

Tonight a dead man would walk among them.

20

Coffee cups were flung everywhere, and sugar cubes were buried under folders. Strangely, none of the cups were broken.

"As though someone was very careful," said Davis as he straightened out the coffee things.

Langton helped clean up, but he did not speak. They were in the office Portakabin to get ready for a meeting of the entire team.

"I suppose this is another thing you'll want to keep secret," Davis said pointedly.

Langton surprised him. "It doesn't matter, Davis. Not now."

"I simply can't see how we can continue." Mandy was speaking. She wrung her hands as she spoke. "I hate to stop, as we all do. And I know we'll all start working again as soon as—"

As soon as what? Davis wondered.

"As soon as we can," she finished. She looked around for support, and the team nodded agreement, although it was clearly not a happy decision.

The entire crew had gathered in the main cabin, except for Jane. She had evidently made her resignation effective immediately.

It was the morning after the generator exploded. Peter was more composed now, but had little to say. He shook out his packet of tobacco and smoked, not looking at anyone.

"We've been happy at times," said Mandy. "Working here together." She seemed dissatisfied with herself. "It's not wrong to stop for a while, until some questions can be answered."

Mr. Langton looked deflated. He shook his head from time to time, and blew air out of his mouth. His white hair was wispier than ever, and for the first time his tie was askew.

"It's Alf, really. If his accident hadn't happened, we'd all feel different about this." Mandy stopped again, and looked around.

"That's right," said Oliver. Other workers nodded, too, and only Skip scowled and seemed to disagree.

Skip glanced at his mates, and held forth his hand, as though begging for reason. "I could keep working myself, like, but what good would it do, one man? I need men working with me, don't I?"

Oliver cleared his throat. "People have been saying you can see the Skeldergate Man some nights. Walking Walmgate Stray. Stalking Hob Moor." Oliver shrugged. "That's what they say."

Mr. Langton sat back in his chair. "We may as well stop," he said. "There's no use pretending. There's something very wrong here."

The workers had apparently expected Langton to insist that they keep working. His agreement with them brought forth murmurs of "We'll be working here again, soon" and "It's only for a short while."

"It's not so very wrong, Mr. Langton," said Oliver. "And we don't really blame you or anyone. Everything will get sorted out, and then we'll all come back."

Everyone was being brave, but no one would pick up a shovel, thought Davis.

"I don't even want to mention this," said Langton. "Perhaps it's unwise. But my wife has told me that things have begun moving about in our house."

The team stared, stunned.

Langton spoke to the floor, as though ashamed. "Teapot, smashed. A picture, sailing off its hook. Nothing terrifying, you understand. But I wish it were not happening, and I think we should stop work here for a while. What do you say, Davis?" Langton asked.

All eyes turned to Davis.

Davis had sat with Irene and Langton in the waiting room all night, while surgeons worked on reattaching Alf's hand. The news was not encouraging. The surgeons had not met their eyes, and all they could get was a "too early to tell."

Dr. Higg was doing badly, too. His blood pressure was shockingly low, and his heart beat as slowly, Dr. Hall reported, as a man who was freezing to death. Medically, Dr. Hall had confided, it all made very little sense. They had him attached to an IV, and monitored his brain and his heart, but medicine was a mere spectator at a time like this.

Now Davis was expected to have something smart to say.

Davis stood and told the team about Alf and Dr. Higg, and explained that the police were working hard on finding the Skeldergate Man, but with no results as yet. The faces Davis saw around him told him that Davis was the leader here now, and that they all counted on him to reassure them, and to make sense out of what was happening.

"I don't blame you if you want to stop working for a while. I'll keep working myself, though. I'm basically a very stubborn person. Besides, I think that our stopping here will not necessarily make the strange events cease. I think we may have unleashed something here, and until we put it to rest it won't stop."

This sounded very possible, but it was hardly reassuring. Irene smiled and nodded. Go on, she seemed to say. You're right.

"Someone has to discover why these things are happening, or they may get worse." Davis saw only pained faces. Surely not, they seemed to say. How could things be worse?

Peter exhaled smoke and watched Davis. The walk the night before had been a success. Hob Moor had been dark, and the long grass wet. He had lingered near a row of houses, bright-lit bedroom windows and back gardens of brussels sprouts and just-turned earth.

And if a few children, a few drunken hooligans, had spied him in the distance, this was exactly what he had wanted. It fit his plan perfectly. That was exactly why he had chosen the moor. "Hob" was an old word for goblin. Many people recalled from their infancy the whispered tales that the moor was haunted.

Let the word spread. The Man walks. Let Davis think about this, and let it eat a hole in him.

But there were voices in his head, a tangle of whispers. The faces around him were colorless through a haze of his own scrambled thoughts. He could hardly hear the voices when they spoke.

The scratch the gray cat had made must have become infected. Cats were such filthy-clawed creatures. Like Davis, they seemed impeccable, but were not. Peter had splashed some gin on it, the only antiseptic he had in the flat, aside from some Gino aftershave from Superdrug.

Soon he would be finished practicing on cats, and ready for larger, more clumsy game. But he would have to concentrate more. Now Davis was asking him a question. Peter pieced it together. "I don't know what I'm going to do," said Peter. He knew one thing. That explosion had frightened him. A machine like a generator did not explode like that.

But already the explosion was fading in his mind. There were so many voices in his head, so many promising schemes.

Peter tried to remember what people had been saying around him. Davis had said something. Something about having nothing else to do.

Peter wanted to laugh, and he nearly did. He would find something for Davis to do.

But faces were waiting for him to speak. He had spoken, hadn't he? He had said he didn't know what he was going to do. That was a clear statement, wasn't it? What did people want? "I don't know," said Peter. "I don't know what I will do." He said this with exaggerated clarity. That should make it clear to them that he did not want to talk, and he did not want to listen.

If only it were quiet.

After the meeting, Mandy stepped beside Peter. She took his hand, and told him something that he didn't quite understand through the buzz of voices in his mind.

"A ghastly time," she said. "And that poor Alf, with his hand."

Peter nodded. Poor Alf.

"It's no wonder you're so upset," she was saying.

Poor Alf. Poor Davis. Davis was going to find something very important to do very soon.

"We should go flying," Mandy was saying. "You used to tell

128

me about your cars and your airplanes. It's not so cold that we couldn't go out this afternoon."

All those voices.

Mandy's presence did quiet the voices somewhat. He could hear her clearly, and that was something. He reflected on what she had suggested.

"You seem so awfully tired, Peter," she said.

The site was empty now. Everyone had gone but Davis and Irene, who stood near Trench One.

"Everyone," she was saying, "needs a holiday now and then."

They walked together for a while. Ducks made slender, V-shaped wakes on the Ouse. A crew was rowing in the distance. The clouds were bright white and off gray. There was only a slight wind, from the west.

"You don't think, do you," she asked, "that there is anything really very sinister about all this?"

He did not answer. Her voice did quiet his mind. It stilled the tangle of voices, all those little boys using words like *nasty* and *naughty* and saying that they see what is happening.

Her soft voice. "I mean anything—and now I hate to use the word. Anything supernatural."

When he added up the costs of the equipment, the heat gun and the soldering iron and the spare engines and fuel pumps, he had over a thousand pounds worth of investment. He told her she could pick the plane she wanted to fly, and she selected a Galaxy Silver Cloud.

"But you don't think that's the best one, do you?" she said.

"No—here. Take this one. The red one. The Boddington Spitfire." It was a handsome model, with a wingspan of over half a meter.

They carried it, the voices mere whispers now, along the Ouse, over stiles, and up to a place where there were only cows, beyond the Ring Road, out where it was not York anymore, and the Minster was a stipple on the horizon.

Peter trembled. What had happened to him over the last weeks? His mind was clear now.

What had happened to me?

He wanted to ask her: Mandy? What have I done?

But she wouldn't know about the cats. Cats. Had he really done that? That was the old Peter, the Peter of his teenage years. He was thirty-eight now, and he had outgrown all that old sickness years before.

Hadn't he?

This was his fastest plane. It could take off in less than three meters of flat ground. Peter found a place where it could taxi for a while. Mandy laughed, and it was more fun to see it bouncing. Then he powered up, the hot-oil whiff of fuel exhaust in the air. It was up hard—he nearly stalled. The plane banked into the wind.

The controls were a black box, looking much like a radio. Mandy said that she wanted to try, and he let her. The controls had a single antenna, but there was nothing simple about them. An Apex computer combo, it had pulse-code modulation so a random signal from another transmitter somewhere would not interfere with Peter's commands.

The plane staggered in the wind high above them, but Mandy could put it through its paces. Peter showed her how to adjust the pitch-trim control slightly. The Spitfire looked black now, it was so high.

Mandy learned minute by minute. The plane banked, slipped, corrected. Peter soared with it in his mind. The green quilt of Ryedale swung before him.

The antenna glinted in the afternoon. At 35 megahertz, Mandy had the plane on an invisible harness, nearly like controlling its .5 diesel engine with a breath, or with a thought. Its propeller gleamed with sun for an instant.

His hand stretched forth and took the controls from her. "I was just finally learning how they worked," she said.

The voices. He spun the plane downward, letting it fall in tight circles, then he brought it out of the spin, powered up, and then cut the throttle.

The voices. So naughty. She's such a very nasty girl, isn't she, this big saucy naughty girl. Take those controls away from that nasty, naughty girl. You know what she likes to do.

He brought the red Spitfire low over the cultivated field. The clods had been plowed just recently, and the white clouds hovered over all of it, as though the world held its breath.

Nasty girl.

The plane whipped across the field, and she squealed, and laughed. It missed her, its engine a loud crack as it went past. It was going so fast it was tiny in the distance as he brought it around. She thought it was fun. She thought it was a kind of sport. Peter backed away from her.

"Peter."

The Spitfire was just off the tops of the grass. There—it cut some of the weeds. He eased it up a few centimeters, just enough to whisk the tussocks of grass. The burr swelled to a loud whine.

"Peter!"

He laughed.

This time it got her, and glanced away, the engine losing power and growling, then surging upward, and cutting way back around in a beautiful turn. It took less time now because the impact had slowed the plane. It came in on a higher arc, not an arc, really, so much as a straight line.

She fell to the ground and it nearly smacked the grass. He brought it up just in time.

"It's not funny, Peter. Give me that."

It came from behind as she snatched, and missed, and tried to grip the antenna, which of course she could not do. The wings expanded in size until they were right behind her head and the engine howled. Her eyes grew wide, reading in Peter's eyes what was about to happen.

The air was littered with flying parts, propeller, struts, engine, hair.

And blood, blood everywhere, all over the dirt, and all over Peter's arms, and even his face, and on his lips, hot salt that he licked.

Blood.

Then he remembered. The terrible thing he had struggled to forget all day came back to him, and he fell to his hands and knees in horror.

The blood before him went gray as his vision dimmed. He closed his eyes.

In his flat last night he had made a terrible discovery.

21

Irene and Davis wandered the dig. It was a lonely place now. Even Peter had slouched off with Mandy, and Davis wished he could spend the day working with a trowel at the bottom of one of the trenches.

Irene was too quiet, and then Davis discovered why. "I must go to London for a few days, Davis," she said, sounding much more subdued than usual.

He looked away. This was the worst possible time for news like this. "I'll miss you," he said raggedly.

"I can tell you are annoyed with me. But I am an editor, with important responsibilities for the next issue, and I have done no work at all. I wish I could stay here."

"I want you to do well," said Davis, trying to sound cheerful, "and be proud of your work, and then I want you to come back to me."

"It is only two hundred miles. Only two hours by train, Davis. I am supposed to be there for four weeks. It is in my contract. But I will do what must be done, and I will return. They will not be able to prevent me."

"Why are you trying to reassure me?"

"Because I can see how you love me."

From any other woman he had ever known this statement would have been embarrassing, or even, conceivably, annoying. But it was true. He loved her. He had not formulated those words, even in his own mind, but there it was, as clearly as if he had seen it on a passing newsstand: DAVIS LOVES IRENE.

"And of course you have guessed by now that I love you, Davis. I don't want to leave you. Not even for a minute. But I will come back."

The railway station was crowded, Davis supposed, but he didn't really see anyone else. He was bewildered by the confusion of such good news and such bad news all at once. Irene loved him. This neon message was the world to Davis now. And yet she carried a backpack and a large leather purse. Her train was due in three minutes. He saw only Irene, with her dark eyes and her smile. Even sad, as she was now, she expressed herself with a smile.

The Intercity One-Twenty-Five rumbled into the station. Brakes squealed. Hands reached from windows to open doors. They were surrounded by passengers and suitcases.

Davis kissed her. He whispered into her ear, so she could hear over the announcements. "Come back soon. I love you."

"I will come back, Davis. Don't worry. Look at me. Why am I so sad to be going for a few days? Only a few days, and only to London. Why am I so sad?"

Perhaps, thought Davis after she was gone, you know something.

York seemed an empty place, or worse. The Minster hulked above the surrounding streets, like a presence that would soon begin to move, and slowly consume all that lay around it. The medieval streets were greasy with wet, although it had not rained for two or three days. People turned away from each other, crouched in dark brown or dark blue wool clothing. A hunched figure sold the *Evening Press,* and Davis bought a copy.

He was not reading idly. He wanted to know how secret the missing Man was at this point. And he wondered—who else thinks they have seen him, wandering the dark? But the disappearance of the Man was still, it seemed, a secret. There was only the usual string of hooliganism and minor thefts. There was a strike in a prison near Leeds, with prisoners refusing to climb down from the roof, and someone seemed to be killing cats in the Clifton district of York.

Davis had tea and a scone in Betty's, and he knew that all the while he was stalling. There was work to do, and there was no one else on the job but one man. Only Davis Lowry. Everyone else had gone away, to protect themselves.

They were not cowards. They were wise. Davis believed that the spirit, if that was the name for it, worked its way inside a person, or a thing, and pressured it until it found a weakness—physical, as perhaps with Dr. Higg, or mental, as perhaps with Davis himself, with the recurrence of his dream. He was certainly not strong enough to withstand a psychological siege.

Or was he? Perhaps he would choose to be strong. It was not a time to be afraid. He believed what he had said. If the source of the troubles was not discovered, they would only grow worse.

There was a crash.

A scone rolled toward Davis, and a long brown snake of tea wended its way across the carpet. A waitress stooped to pick up the tray.

Someone had dropped some dishes. The sort of thing, Davis reassured himself, that happens every day. A routine accident.

There was no reason to be disturbed. He repeated to himself: a routine accident.

He hurried from the tea shop.

The door to Foote's Book Shop was locked. Davis pushed the button, and then leaned on it. There was no answer, and he wondered if the button was connected to anything.

He turned away, cursing to himself, and then a squeak of hinge made him turn back. Mr. Foote's pale, irritated face glanced up and down the street, and then saw Davis bearing down upon him.

"I don't have time!" yelped Mr. Foote, but he allowed Davis to climb the stairs behind him. "I'm in the midst of a catastrophe!"

There was a sound of heavy rain, a squall. But it came from above them, within the building. The carpet on the steps was black with water. Each step was sloppy. Water made a high-pitched toneless song somewhere in the building.

It burst from a small bathroom in a corner. Heavy plumber's tools and basins and rags were everywhere, but a spray still danced from a joint beneath a sink. Mr. Foote had apparently decided to move books instead of fighting the burst pipe. He had columns of books on chairs and stools.

Davis wrestled with the joint. A heavy black wrench slipped, and slipped again, ringing loudly against the pipe. Davis was soaked. Another wrench was too small. Davis managed, using a succession of wrong-sized wrenches or spanners—or whatever, he muttered to himself, the stupid iron insufficiencies were called—to stop the leak.

He sat in a pond. It was very quiet without the incessant scream of water.

The two men mopped, and squeezed water into buckets. At last the wettest damage was cleaned up, and Davis sat before a radiator in the next room, warming himself and drying his clothes.

Mr. Foote made some tea, and collapsed into a chair. "I am grateful for your help," said Mr. Foote. "Extremely grateful. I wouldn't have let you in except for the fact that I had called for a plumber. He'll no doubt arrive sometime tomorrow."

Mr. Foote sipped his tea and made a face. Still too hot, he mouthed. "This was the strangest disaster I have ever seen. The pipe simply exploded. There's no reason for it to do that. I nearly lost thousands of pounds worth of architecture books. They are my most expensive sort of book, with the exception of some of the eighteenth-century botanical prints."

"There was no reason for it to do that?"

"None at all."

Davis explained that he had heard this sort of comment before. He told the story of the generator. "Even now, I don't know if they will be able to save the hand. I know they can work wonders, but the surgeons did not seem very optimistic."

Mr. Foote absorbed this news unhappily.

"You must tell me everything you know about Skeldergate," Davis urged. "Not simply the very old. But the more recent. I want to know why the owners of the warehouse there decided to move. And how long the buildings stood empty before anyone made a move to tear them down. Were there unusual injuries during the demolition? I want to know how many little crimes have happened there, within living memory. I need to know everything. There is only one thing that can defeat this, whatever it is. Knowledge. I need information."

"You know enough," said Mr. Foote. "You know a king's body was dumped there, without ceremony. Because of this brutal contempt for his remains, the spirit is vengeful. If you want me to speak plainly, I have done so. Must I simplify it any more for you? The site is extremely dangerous to everyone who has even the slightest contact with it. Now that you have spoken to me, I am tangled up in whatever powers emanate from the unholy place, and that is why my pipes burst. I don't need a plumber, I need a priest. Please go away, Mr. Lowry. You are a very dangerous man."

"I need to know what to do."

"I suppose I should write a simple instruction book with frightening drawings for you so you could understand. I am afraid. I am very frightened. I am terrified, and I want you to go away. The situation is beyond what mere knowledge can cure."

"What do you suggest?"

"Go away from here. As far away as possible."

Davis was glad to be back in the street. He passed a man in gray work clothes looking at the numbers beside various doors. Davis directed him to Foote's shop, and then walked quickly across Deangate, and across the Minster green, to the Minster Library.

Davis asked to be admitted to the room with the rare manuscripts. "It's extremely important."

No one moved to help him. "You must be Mr. Lowry," said a large man with a beard. "I was told that you might possibly pay us a visit. Mr. Langton has left a message for you. He would like you to ring him immediately."

Davis was mystified, but used the telephone in the well-organized office.

"Stop whatever you are doing and come over here at once," said Langton. This peremptory tone was very much unlike Langton. His voice sounded hoarse, close to hysteria.

"How did you know I was going to show up here?"

"At once, Davis. I must see you now."

"My work here was only going to take a few minutes."

"Now, Davis. Please."

Davis hesitated before the door to the rare manuscripts. "Actually," said the bearded man, "he also asked us to not, under any circumstances, let you use any of our manuscripts."

The man offered this not simply as a way of forbidding entry. He was plainly extremely curious, and wondered if Davis might be a terrorist, or a madman.

Three other librarians eyed him from the desks.

136

Davis smiled, and the man returned his smile, with some misgivings. "Perhaps the confusion can be sorted out."

"I left messages everywhere. All the museums. All the libraries. I need to talk with you."

Mr. Langton looked collected enough. He wore a gray cardigan, and a green knit tie. Mrs. Webster brought in tea, and Langton made a great show of fussing over which sugar cube to use. Davis declined tea. Langton shook his head, very slightly. He did not like this. It was a bad way to start a meeting, and it was apparently a meeting that Langton had planned. A meeting between the two of them. A meeting that would hold, for Davis, bad news. "I wanted to talk to you before you could do anything."

"What was it you thought I was about to do?"

"Nothing in particular. Anything in general. I wanted to stop you in your tracks, and this is what I have done."

"Why?"

"No need to be irritated, Davis."

Davis waited.

"I admire you, as you must know."

Davis forced a pleasant expression onto his face.

"You are the only one of our entire side who wants to keep up the fight. Admirable."

Davis would not make this easy for Langton. Davis did not speak, and he did not take one of the little yellow biscuits Langton pushed toward him.

"I want you to stop. I want you to take a short holiday. Go to London, perhaps. Or up to Edinburgh. Go somewhere, and do nothing."

Davis stared.

"Or if you insist on staying here, do absolutely nothing regarding our dig here. Do not go into the lab. Do not go near the site. Do nothing. You understand me, I hope."

"You forbid me."

"Please don't use such naked phrases, Davis."

"But you do forbid me."

"At the end of the day, I am responsible for you, for Irene, for Mandy, Jane—for all of you. Every one of you. And our work here is stirring up this—this evil, you might say. Like making a hive of bees upset. If we calm down and turn to other matters, perhaps

137

the—the evil—perhaps the unfortunate events—perhaps they might stop taking place, and there is no reason to stare at me like that, Davis."

Davis stood.

"So you will turn to other matters for a while, won't you, Davis?"

"Knowledge is what we need. Not ignorance. Forthrightness. Not cowardice."

"Well put, Davis, but you have a very small audience to sway, an audience of one, and I am not moved."

Davis studied this bland man, realizing that he had never paid him much attention. Langton was a man who, like so many Englishmen behind desks, looked vague and preoccupied with detail, and he certainly lacked Dr. Higg's humanity. He was a colorless man, and he was a man you would easily lose in a crowd. He did know one thing very well. He knew how to say no.

Davis resented Langton, and he would, naturally, not follow the bureaucrat's instructions. But he had a grudging respect for what was, in this officious man, a certain toughness. He would thank Langton and say nothing more.

The telephone trilled, and Langton spoke briefly.

He hurried from behind his desk, and flung himself into a coat.

"Come with me, Davis. Something ghastly is happening."

22

Alf was strapped into his bed. He cried out, but his words were impossible to understand, if they were words at all.

Gradually, though, Davis could understand them. "Get away from me! Please, get away from me!"

Again and again, imploring someone or something to leave him alone.

"I see him," said Alf, his thick tongue making his words nearly indistinguishable. "I see him, at the window."

There was a window there, beside Alf. Grass, and the trunk of a tree.

Nurses hurried in and hurried out. Davis took one look at Alf, and had to hang on to something—he found a chair to lean on. Langton trembled, and had to sit down. A nurse attended to him, putting a hand on his forehead, bringing him a glass of water.

Alf groaned and tossed. He glistened with sweat. His tongue was swollen and filled his mouth, brown and quaking, like a toad. The worst thing about this appearance, however, was his eyes. They had sunk far into his skull, and when his lids trembled open, there was nothing but dark holes.

The injured arm was a great white melon of bandages. The arm had been strapped into place, but it jerked from time to time. Dr. Hall strode into the room, and gazed down at the thrashing figure. He glanced at Langton, and then crooked a finger at Davis.

"His nervous system is necrotizing," said Dr. Hall. "The major nerves are simply disintegrating. I say 'simply.' It isn't simple at all. I've never seen anything like it. The optic nerve is already gone. Dissolved, like so much overcooked porridge."

"It has nothing to do with the explosion, does it?"

Dr. Hall pulled at his lower lip. He roused himself as though from a daze. "There's a law in medicine, as in every other science. I think of it as the Uniqueness Prohibition. If it happens in one place, it happens in many, is one way of putting it. There are rare syndromes, nearly unheard-of diseases. But virtually nothing that is literally unique. What is happening to this man is unheard of. What is happening to Dr. Higg is equally mystifying, although quite different. Both men are suffering from something apparently unique."

"I think we should have a talk," said Davis.

Dr. Hall gave him a hard look. "Yes, I think we should."

"It will take a few minutes. I can't explain it all here. You won't believe it, anyway."

Dr. Hall smiled, and Davis liked him. The man did not mind mysteries. What he really minded was death. "Let's take a quick walk, shall we? We can have some fresh air and some privacy at the same time."

The District Hospital grounds were bright in the afternoon, and the trees, while black and bare, seemed to be tipped with the lightest gold from place to place. Naked rose stalks shivered on their stakes, and the earth was black where a gardener had worked it. It was winter and spring at once, and the green of the lawns as the two men talked was shocking, nearly unbelievable, as though the tint control on a television set overadjusted to produce a blazing green impossible in nature. There was a scent of wet earth, and, far away, the purr of a lawn mower.

Dr. Hall did not even ask a question until Davis had told everything, even the tale of the burst pipe in Mr. Foote's bookshop, and then Dr. Hall shook his head sadly. "How could so many bright people suffer such a delusion?"

Davis was irritated, but then he realized that Dr. Hall was

140

reacting as any rational person would, as Davis himself would have reacted a few weeks ago.

"Now that you have lost all respect for us," said Davis, with as much cheer as he could, "I suppose you still have no idea what is wrong with Alf and Dr. Higg."

Dr. Hall shook his head. "Your interesting story has shed no light at all. We're wasting time, as well."

As though to demonstrate the truth of this, a nurse stood in the distance, waving a white arm. The two men ran, and the nurse told them with a glance that something very bad was happening.

Alf's face was shriveled, gray and nearly unrecognizable. The skin of his uninjured arm was so withered that the tattoos had lost much of their definition. Black fluid streamed from Alf's nostrils.

Dr. Hall swore, and snapped instructions. Alf heaved against the restraints. For several minutes nurses and doctors wrestled with the struggling figure.

Alf howled, and his head seemed to burst.

Black, putrid matter spattered the ceiling and the walls, and Alf gave a long, broken groan.

He was silent.

Then the men and women slumped, fatigued. The body did not move. Dr. Hall gave quiet instructions, and turned to face Davis.

The doctor was thin and small suddenly. He looked away from Davis, and yet seemed to need to talk.

Davis had enough experience with postmortems to be able to hazard a guess or two. Alf had apparently suffered a massive infection that had attacked the nervous tissues. Davis had handled a number of skulls of syphilis victims. A massive infection could even eat into the bone of the skull, rotting it as worms rot wood. But syphilis took decades to accomplish its horror. This had taken hours.

Dr. Hall sighed and shook his head, indicating that he couldn't talk just yet. He gazed at the floor, and then turned angrily away from Davis, as though Davis reminded him of ghosts and poltergeists and other such foolishness.

It was hard to believe that cheerful, lively Alf was gone.

A fellow worker. A colleague.

Someone who needed to be avenged.

Mr. Langton had watched it all, and now sat with his arms

folded. "They weren't much use, were they, all these well-trained people."

One of the nurses glanced his way. She was using a white rag on some of the debris that had burst from Alf's body.

"They did their best, though," Langton added quickly. "Admirable people."

The older man stood weakly, and put his hand to the chair for support. Then he shook himself. "We mustn't give in to weakness, must we?"

Davis could think only, Alf is gone.

"Peter will be shocked," said Davis at last. "He thought we would save Alf, even his hand. Peter's already pretty disturbed by all of this. This will be hard."

"Peter knew something like this would happen," said Langton. "He knew someone would die."

Figures ran in the corridor.

"Another casualty," said Langton vaguely.

Then the two of them hurried, too.

The crisis was in Dr. Higg's room.

A tall, heavyset nurse blocked the door. They would have no more criticism from Mr. Langton. "Just a minute, if you please," she said.

Dr. Higg was wheeled out of his room, a tangle of transparent tubes and medical personnel. Davis could see only a glimpse of Higg's ashen profile.

"You see, Davis, what we are up against," said Langton, when he could speak.

Davis did not. What they were up against was entirely mysterious, although apparently malevolent and extremely powerful. Beyond that, he knew nothing. He had the bare beginnings of a plan, though. A sketchy plan. He needed information, and time.

"This is why we must stop working on anything associated with Skeldergate," said Langton. "Perhaps we may even have to fill in the trenches."

Davis wheeled, appalled. "And destroy all that work!"

Alf's work.

"Try not to hate me, Davis. None of us believe in such things. The Bible has its witch of Endor and other such devils and demons. So perhaps it's not unchristian to believe in such things. I really

142

don't know what to believe. I know only one thing, Davis: there's nothing at all we can do."

We shall see, thought Davis.

The Minster Library would close in half an hour. It was nearly dark in late afternoon. The Minster cast not only a shadow, but a dark that spilled everywhere, filling the sky.

"I require admission into the rare manuscript room. Not as a staff member of the Foundation. On my own business."

Davis flashed his cards identifying him as a member of three different university faculties—two of the cards were out of date, but there was no need to explain that. There was one of Dr. Higg's cards expressing hope that "all courtesies would be extended," a card Davis had carried for some fifteen years, and never had to use until now.

The bearded librarian frowned. It was all too complicated, he seemed to be thinking. Americans with little white cards. The world was cluttered with them.

Another librarian, a woman, smiled up at Davis. "I saw you on television. It was on BBC Two. I begin to remember—it was a few years ago. I seem to remember you from—was it 'Open University'?"

"That's right," said Davis. "My lecture on the nasal index."

"Nasal index! And you want to see our manuscripts?"

"Just briefly."

Davis climbed the ladder, located the volume, and leaped down. Gentle with the ancient pages, but as quickly as he could, he found the place he wanted and tilted the pages to get the best light.

The ancient script was nearly invisible in places. He searched back in the chronicle, discovering what had happened to previous kings, how they had died, and most important, how they had been buried. Plainly, being a king was a temporary position in York's eighth century. There had been plots and counterplots, and the kings had not been, in the best of times, particularly powerful.

The deaths of ancient kings, and ancient lords. "In the ninth month of his reign the ring-giver, lord of Bodeton and the Oak Ford, and lord of the Kingdom north of the Humber, died by the grace of God almighty, and was buried with his sword."

143

"In that month a great water rose from the west and fell upon the lands, with a great foulness, and many lords fell by the will of God almighty, and were buried with their swords."

So many people, faded to tea-pale smudges on a sheepskin page.

He called Irene from the Phonecard booth near the Lendal Bridge.

"Poor Alf," said Irene. "The doctor looked like such a determined man. No doubt he is very unhappy."

Everyone was unhappy, said Davis. "I suppose Mr. Langton is the most upset of all. He has forbidden me to do any more work on the dig, or to have anything to do with investigating what has been happening."

"But you will not stop working, will you?"

The little window in the telephone showed that his Phonecard credits were nearly used up.

He wished she were here, this moment. He had an instant sense of her smile, and her body, her perfect black hair, the curve of her under him, her breath at his ear.

"You will not give up, Davis, because you know that you are right."

There was a note taped to the door of his flat. "Call Mr. Langton."

Davis used the coin phone near the abbey walls. There was only a recorded message at the office, Mrs. Webster telling Davis what to do at the sound of the tone. Davis hung up, and fed the telephone twenty pence. This time Mrs. Langton answered at the Langton residence.

"A terrible thing, Mr. Lowry. I don't even want to say."

Worse, Davis wanted to ask, than what had already happened that day?

Mr. Langton would pick him up. He should stay where he was, and wait not five minutes.

Langton drove quickly, which, Davis imagined, was not like him. The city was entirely dark now, and the headlights of Langton's Ford did not seem to succeed against the black.

144

"Not a pretty business," was all Langton would say.
Davis had to nearly beg for information.
"Two matters, really," said Langton.
Langton swerved to miss a man on a bicycle.
"Should I try to guess?"
"You couldn't. The first one is, perhaps, fairly simple. Did Mandy mention going off anywhere? Down to London, perhaps, with Irene?"
"No, not at all."
"Well, she's gone missing, then. She was supposed to lecture at Saint Andrews tonight on Norse artifacts uncovered at the dig. She's a charming speaker, and enjoys it, and she can use the money."
"Sick, perhaps. Or maybe she forgot."
"Mmmm," doubtfully. "Perhaps."
There was a long silence. They were well out of York now, heading southwest, as nearly as Davis could tell.
"Bishopthorpe," said Langton in answer to Davis's question. "Closer to Acaster Malbis, actually."
"Could you, maybe, give me just a hint as to what is happening?"
Langton sighed, and as frustrated as Davis felt, he decided not to push the man.
"Not a pretty business," said Langton after driving silently for a moment. "When was the last time you saw Jane Hull?"
Davis didn't know. He had thought—perhaps Mandy had told him—that she was quitting and leaving for London.
"Yes, I knew that. We had a word. She thought this project might not be the best thing for her career. Can't imagine anyone thinking that, can you?" he added, a bit of dry humor that Davis appreciated, even as it surprised him.
"This will certainly be the pinnacle of my résumé, for as long as I live," said Davis.
Langton drove, every furlong that they traveled just that much closer to exactly the sort of thing Langton most wanted to avoid. He found himself resenting Higg for spending all this time completely unconscious. Langton was capable, but he was not intended for the slings and arrows of fortune quite this outrageous.
"I am beginning to become rather familiar with the police," said Langton at last. "After years of television, I'm afraid I am a little disappointed."

Davis began to guess what had happened. He could not, naturally, imagine the details. But he, too, wished the car would blow a tire, or that the calendar could shift and find them all just a few weeks before all this—anything to delay what was about to happen.

Davis did not bother to ask any more questions. He didn't want to know.

Lights swung on the black water. Blue police lights flashed, and electric torches illuminated reeds, then water, then road as their bearers turned their attention from one place to another.

"We had her and then we lost her," said a policeman.

"How, exactly," asked Mr. Langton, "did you manage that?"

Bubbles burst on the surface of the river.

"Our divers brought up a handbag. Here it is. Here's a library ticket with her name on it."

"Yes, but you haven't a body?"

"We thought we did."

Langton turned to Davis and, although the two men could not see each other's features, there was a moment of shared exasperation.

"It's dark, you see, and she's hard to get a hold of. I do want to apologize. We should have her any moment now."

"Lovely," muttered Langton.

Langton and Davis walked to the edge of the darkness. A van with a loud generator backed to the edge of the river, and the scene was illuminated with nearly blinding blue light. Policemen parted bushes, and the frogmen rose, spitting water, and clearing mouthpieces. "Nowt yet," said one. The river water looked green in the unnatural light.

Langton put his hands into his pockets. "They think," he said, "they have Jane's body."

23

The lights glittered on the water, and the frogmen rose and adjusted their face masks. Their black wet suits were smeared with light, and the mouthpieces to their aqualungs were bright yellow. They consulted with each other, and sank again, strewing the water and white stars.

The river was full with early spring runoff. Eddies and countereddies churned the surface. At times the river looked like the muscles of a massive, running beast.

It was not a warm night. "Fresh," one young policeman said to another. "It is that," the other said.

Langton fumed. "Bloody hell," he muttered. "I've never seen anything to equal this. They expect us to watch them make a total cock-up of whatever it is they think they're doing. 'We'll need you,' they said, 'to verify the identity of the body.' So we have to stand here and watch this."

The policemen grew from apologetic to taciturn to vaguely hostile.

"Shouldn't be long now," one would say.

"We'll have it up in no time at all now," said another.

And another, "You can't hurry this sort of thing."

And at last, "It's foolish to try to hurry the men along. No need to worry. We'll have questions for you when we're done."

This last was threatening somehow. "I believe," said Langton at last, "that we may as well leave. It's after midnight."

None of the police encouraged them to stay.

Langton drove. An owl hovered before them in the headlights, and then twisted and was gone.

"Maybe they won't find her," said Davis.

"Some children saw a body. The police fished out a handbag, and one of the divers claimed to have seen her down in the muck. Or some sort of body. The police are not terribly impressive, are they?"

"Not terribly."

"I want the keys," said Langton, his voice suddenly hard.

"Keys?"

"Don't pretend to be deaf. The keys to the laboratory. I want them."

"I have them here in my pocket."

"That's very convenient, then."

"Are you planning to do some research tonight?"

"I'll take them now, if you please."

"I can't help wondering why you want them."

"To prevent you from going there. I'll take them now."

"Absolutely not. I have property of my own in that lab, notebooks and software, and I have a right to have access to things that belong to me."

"This is going to be unpleasant. I can prevent you from entering that lab, can't I? By force of law?"

"Let's make it pleasant. I'll use the key tonight, remove all my personal possessions, and only my own possessions, and give you the keys the first thing tomorrow."

Besides, thought Davis, the work I have to do there will take only an hour or two.

"I find it difficult to trust you. I know you plan some sort of heroic effort. I have no idea what. I can see it in the way you set your jaw. I forbid any such attempts to be brilliant, Davis. The most brilliant man I know is near death in hospital. Brilliance doesn't impress me."

"I'll make a serious effort not to be brilliant."

148

"I don't want to see you strapped into a hospital bed," said Langton, softening his voice.

"I'll give you the keys first thing tomorrow."

"This may be very foolish."

"What can possibly happen?"

"I don't know what's been happening all along, do I? All I know is that one man is dead, and possibly a woman, and the first thing I'll have to do when I reach home is ring the duty nurse to see if William is still alive. This has all made me a little less keen on scientific research."

Langton dropped Davis off at the lab, and did not bother warning him or urging him to display common sense. He turned away, and jerked the Ford into the street, as though to distance himself at once from Davis's stubborn foolishness.

Davis, alone now, his feeling of mild triumph over Langton fading, took the keys from his pocket. Langton was right, in a conservative, administrative way. And Langton wasn't such a worthless man. He had displayed no small amount of pluck during this long day.

Dr. Higg, lying comatose, with three or four heartbeats per minute, like a man freezing to death. Alf, exploding with the blackness that had eaten his nerves.

Necrotizing.

They had her library ticket.

What had Alf seen at the hospital window?

Irene's faith in him pulled him across the stepping stones. He unlocked doors, and climbed down stairs, and turned on the lights in the lab. Now that he was here he did not want to stay.

It had always been too cold. The fluorescent lights buzzed. The finds trays were all put away, and drawers marked ARTEFACTS—the spelling in use here—were shut and locked, with a computer printout cataloging each find Irene had processed so far.

Davis gathered his notebooks. They were a small pile, and would be easy to carry. He avoided going into the Skeldergate Man's room until he could not put it off any longer. Even then he made excuses. He had no real reason to open the door to the room. He didn't expect to find anything there.

But these days, he told himself, we don't know what, exactly, to

149

expect. An archaeologist never does. It's best to look into the room, just to make sure.

Make sure of what?

He switched on the light, and the light fluttered, half-on, half-off. There was still a trace of fingerprint powder on the door handle, and on the edge of the bare table. It was more cold than usual in here. His breath was pale at his lips. His ungloved fingers burned with the cold.

He backed out of the room. He was glad to lock it.

Davis switched on the computer. After loading DOS, he loaded the Datamaster system, knowing that he was about to stretch the limits of the duties such software was intended to perform. He searched under the keyword ROYAL and, not to his surprise, came up with nothing. He searched for RELIGIOUS, and coaxed the computer into a list of possible religious objects classified from the Skeldergate site. Some possible amulets, a golden limb which someone had given to a saint in thanks for restoring strength to an arm, and a small Norman cross. Interesting finds, each deserving attention, but not what he needed tonight.

What he needed, what they all needed, was knowledge. How to make everything peaceful again. How to put the badness to rest. It was knowledge that would do it, and knowledge came like this, turning the pages of an ancient volume, blinking at the screen of a computer, quietly, hunting without moving.

BURIAL came up with too many confusing finds. DEATH came up blank.

He punched in the keyword SWORD and got a cluttered list. He punched CEREMONIAL SWORD, and the computer listed only one such weapon, the fine sword hilt Dr. Higg had displayed in London.

Perfect.

There was a sound.

A dragging hiss. Like a plastic sheet tugged across the floor. Like a leather body dragging itself. Pulling itself step by step, down the stairs.

Of course the Man would come back. Of course he would. Where would he go in this entire world but where he had been? He had no imagination. He could only return. Isn't that what the dead do? Return—if they do anything at all?

Stop it. Stop it, you're being childish. You're scaring yourself. There is nothing here, and you know it.

150

Davis switched off the computer, and put the software back in its plastic case. He locked this in its drawer. He surveyed the lab, his notebooks under his arm. Everything is fine, he said to himself. Nothing missing, nothing out of place.

He was stalling. He didn't want to ascend the dark stairs.

He tried to hum a happy tune, because he had always believed in music. He couldn't think of a single tune. His mind was empty. Gradually, little demitunes came back to him, jingles for hair lotion and car dealerships, hardly the sort of music to combat the fear he had now.

It wasn't fear. Fear is a feeling. This was a heaviness in his chest, and a thickness in his throat. The colors of the room were too bright. He was cold, and he wanted to hurl himself into the wall, and through it, into the earth, anywhere, as long as it wasn't here.

The frogmen were searching, even now, stretching forth their hands.

It wasn't a simple matter of imagination. Alf had really died. Of course, there were those dreams, but anything could happen in a dream—absolutely anything. This was not a dream. He was awake, and this was the world.

He could not move. There was a sound, somewhere. Not in the lab, somewhere out there, in the dark.

He swore at himself, and marched himself across the room, and turned out the light. If he stood frozen in imaginative horror like a little boy, there was no telling where his thoughts would lead. True, some bad things had happened. But a forthright attitude, and a good ladling of common sense, was the best way to deal with this sort of situation. Everyone else was afraid. Didn't he have a certain amount of pride?

The stairs were dark. But it was only dark. There was no icy breath at his cheek, no hand on his arm.

Only a long series of stairs, and doors to be locked, and at last the night and the wet grass, and the last key turned, the walk home.

Bushes, trees. A distant streetlight. The bare trembling of a rose bush, all thorns. The night smelled of the soil, and growing things, grass and old leaves becoming earth. It was a lovely smell.

Something moved.

There, between the trees. There was the sound again, the sound of something dragging, limply. And another sound, too, a deter-

151

mined growl, like the wheeze of a man with bad lungs pulling himself along.

With very bad lungs, and the thing was coming closer. He could see the shape of the head rising, and lurching, and lifting again.

Davis ran. He flung himself over a wall, and retrieved the notebook that fluttered to the concrete.

When he looked back there was nothing. He forced himself to look hard, between the trees and the bushes, in the black rectangle of each building. A tree lifted, full of wind for a moment. That was the sound he had heard, the wind in the bony trees.

There was nothing else.

He made a little, unconvinced laugh, a noise like a pebble hitting a stone. Running away from nothing.

He walked up Gillygate, past the black shop windows. The broken fragment of wall that marked the beginning of Bootham was as pale as a wall made of lunar stone.

He trudged by the newsagent. The streetlights made it easy to see that he was not being followed, and besides, what would be following him in the midst of a city like this? There were other people out, even at this hour.

Except, when he looked hard, they were only shadows. He was alone. There were no people. There were no living, and no dead. Only naked trees.

24

He stretched out in his tiny sitting room. Among his notebooks was his small Panasonic, and he listened to himself conduct the postmortem, delighted at the way Irene interrupted him. He rewound parts of it to hear her voice again.

He made himself some toast, and he smeared blackberry jam on the slices of wholewheat. This was bread he ordinarily liked. He had bought it at the whole-food store, where they baked it themselves. But he was too tired to eat. It was a pity he didn't have a telephone. He wished he could talk to her.

Alf exploded, black snakes running out of his nose.

He could not close his eyes without seeing Alf's body twisting against the straps. The doctors had been inept to let that happen. Surely they could have done better than that. Langton's attitude toward doctors and police were that they did not do a very good job. Langton was right. They did a terrible job.

There was a step on the stair. There, just now.

He was too tired to be frightened. He dragged himself to the bedroom, and fell across the bed. Must get up, he told himself. Must turn out the lights. There was a little electric meter behind the

153

kitchen door. If he didn't feed it fifty-pence coins all the electricity would run out.

It would run out, he told himself, and then what would happen? He would put some money into the slot, turn the little handle, and then he would have electricity again. The hot water would be lukewarm, but that only meant he wouldn't take a bath right away. But the curtains were open and this meant the morning light would stream in on him from the east. This would be a problem.

Don't get up. There were no problems, he reassured himself. There was only sleep.

This time in the dream it was night. The water trembled beneath his feet. He walked across the surface of the lake, and the moonlight shuddered on the water. But the lake was too wide now. It was a sea. It was so vast that he could barely see her. She was a tiny dab of light far, far away.

He did not want to call her this time. There was something wrong, but he did not know that. She called him, her voice like a strand of spiderweb in the dark.

Davis. Come to me.

No, thought Davis, and he stopped walking, and the water sagged under him like a cloth, but supported him, rising and falling.

Something wrong. No, I don't want to see you anymore. I can't see you anymore, I have to turn back.

I have to leave. There's something—

Wrong.

He woke. He lay across the bed, shivering. It was over, and he was thankful for that. The dream had been more threatening than ever before. There had been something tainted about it from the beginning, some presence in the dream that had ground against him.

Then he knew what it was.

It was that noise, the same sound that he had heard outside the lab. A low wheezing sound, a sound like very bad lungs working against a great weight. Rising and falling, the grinding noise, this ancient asthmatic wheeze, dragging air in, and pushing it out.

It was a part of the dream, thought Davis. He was still asleep. He sat up. He touched his lips with his fingers. I'm still asleep. He bit a knuckle, just hard enough, and put a hand out to the wall.

Awake.

He was awake, and there was still that noise, and the noise was growing louder. It was still not loud—it was not the sort of noise that would ever be very loud. It was insistent, like the hiss of a step, of someone dragging across the floor. And yet, not like a hiss, either, and it was growing more and more clear.

It was coming closer. Because there really was a sound; there was no question about that now. The sound was real, and he was awake. He wanted to ask: Who's there? He wanted to speak, but to speak would be to admit that something was wrong, and to keep silent would be to say that there wasn't anything wrong at all, just something that didn't make sense.

In the next room. And then not in the next room. In the hall. Something just outside the door, and yet the bedroom door was open. This proved that there was nothing there. If there was something there he would see it by now, because that insistent, relentless step was just there.

Right there.

Now.

The head hunched into the doorway. The light from the kitchen was bright, and gleamed on the ebony leather of its skin, and the clotted textile of its rags. One hand was outstretched, the gilding of the light spilling along it.

Davis could not make a sound. He fought to draw a breath, but he made only a choking noise, and he backed away, crawling backward, and fell off the bed, dragging the bedding with him.

He crawled to his feet, unable to see anything but that lurching figure. He pulled himself along the wall, and the figure followed him. The arm stretched toward him, nearly touching him.

There was another sound, not only the rise and fall of the steps, but an animal, savage cry.

No!

My own voice, thought Davis, and the cry would not stop.

Over and over calling out against what he saw.

The dark fingers touched Davis's lips, and the ancient face was before him, closing on Davis, the sad features, the eyes closed, but not closed he saw, opening, coming closer, nearly on him, the cold breath stale with the flavor of the leathered lungs.

Davis smashed the window with his elbow, and leaped, slicing the backs of his thighs on the glass, smashing through the rest of the window with his head, rolling down the slate roof, still calling that none of this was real. He slipped down the cold slate.

He fell.

And hung on. The drain edge cut into his fingers, but it supported his weight. He gasped, struggling to swing himself back onto the slope of the roof. He knew he could do it. There was the slate, and here was his body, and all he had to do was swing himself up.

The figure stood there at the window, watching.

The drain groaned, and fell away, and he held onto it as it dangled downward, weakening, and yet still suspending him. A trickle of water spattered his face. Then, without a sound, the drain broke free, and he fell.

This time, nothing stopped him.

It took a long time. He had time to remember the black spear-fences that lanced upward everywhere in York. He remembered brick walls with their sharp, unyielding straight edges. But mostly he remembered to steady himself as he fell, wheeling his arms, taking a deep breath as though to scream, wondering with a shock worse than anything he had ever experienced, how long it took to die.

PART Three

25

Langton could not sleep. He was, he supposed, exhausted, but that did not matter. He did not even undress. His wife heated some milk, and the warm milk was quite delicious, but did nothing to encourage him toward bed. There was simply too much happening.

He had always had an overly advanced sense of responsibility. He was responsible for at least some of what had happened. Or, at least, he felt responsible. He should not, for example, have let Higg stay overnight with that ancient leathered mummy. He wished the ancient bag of trouble had never been found. Langton didn't care for dead things anyway, and while he knew such old bog men enthralled the scientists, and won over the hearts and pocketbooks of the public, he had to admit that Irene had, perhaps, the more civilized attitude. He had cringed when he had heard it. Irene was a charming girl, but had this terrible propensity for untimely straightforwardness. But she was right, in her way.

There was something obscene about this love of dead bodies, mummies, and such. He wondered what the Church of England felt about cremation. A good idea, that. A bad few minutes, and then you are so much dust. God will love you just as much if you are a handful of dust. What does He care?

Metaphysics. He was sitting in his favorite chair, mulling metaphysics, and it was—he craned his neck to see the clock—two in the morning. He had rung the nurse—Higg was still alive. Still alive, but still the same, which was to say nearly dead.

He asked Harry, the border collie, if he wanted to go for a walk, and of course the dog indicated that he would.

His wife was half asleep, and murmured something like surprise. "A walk. At this hour?"

"Can't sleep, can I, and who could blame me?"

No one. The last twenty-four hours had been hellish.

The dog was not surprised. Langton was given to fits of sleeplessness. Hardly insomnia, nothing deserving a serious name. Simply a sense of responsibility. A monthly report might keep Langton awake for three consecutive nights. He was, by profession, a worrier.

Langton was not a scientist. He was, at heart, a man who kept things organized. He admired the men and women he worked with, but sometimes felt that he had a point of view somewhat more objective. The romance of ancient things did not wear long with him.

The dog wet this and wet that, trees, gateposts. The two of them strolled to Clifton Green. Cold, naturally. But not so cold. The dog sniffed and snuffled in the grass.

As his wife had heated the milk, Sainsbury's Virtually Fat-Free, she had mentioned something, and it was this small bit of news, in passing, that had killed Langton's sleep more than anything else.

"Someone's done it again," she had said, tilting the milk pan into the cup.

This was an annoying rhetorical device. She knew that Langton lived in perfect ignorance of most of the things that happened in her life, including the vicissitudes of "Neighbours," and all the other fictional crises on television.

"Someone's done it again, and the police haven't a clue."

"The police," he had said, interested in more news of police bungling. "I wonder if they ever do anything right."

"Someone got the big gray tom over on West Parade. Belongs to Mrs. Phillips, who did the Christian Aid last year. Whose house was hit by a thunderbolt that storm we had last year, that bad one?"

"That killed the pigeons in the Museum Gardens?"

"That storm; it was different lightning."

The milk was too hot. Langton told her that he knew who Mrs. Phillips was, and yet knew nothing about her cat.

"Of course, you not liking cats."

"I don't, really. Of course I have nothing against them. Take care of themselves quite well, as a rule."

"But you're a man for dogs."

Langton admitted that she was right, and then pursued the subject of the gray tomcat belonging, when it had belonged to anyone, to Mrs. Phillips. "Is there something wrong with it?"

"In a manner of speaking."

Langton had the same trouble in France. Translating a newspaper into actual information took time. "Is the cat dead?"

"How did you guess that?"

"You told me, I believe."

"I didn't."

"How did it die?"

"The police don't know. They found him floating in the Ouse." The river was pronounced *ooze*. Langton thought of ooze at the bottom of the river, and frogmen.

Jane's white skin.

"But there have been several cats gone missing in the last few weeks," she continued. "And more than one or two found in the river."

Langton admitted that this was a fascinating mystery, and then he could not speak. He had washed his hands, although they had not needed washing, and asked her to repeat all she knew about the missing cats.

"Well, I don't know how they died. Someone killed them, I suppose."

"Poison?"

"I couldn't say, could I?"

Now he watched Harry nuzzle tussocks of grass. If it were poison, then that would be a relief. Because Peter had never used poison. He had used his hands, as Langton recalled. So perhaps someone was poisoning cats, and hurling the bodies into the river.

But would one do that, actually? A poisoner never really knows when the victim has eaten the tainted bit of liver. A poisoner would not throw victims into a river.

How many had she said? He couldn't remember. Enough to

161

cause an interest in the press. There would have been others, then, that no one knew about. He would have to ask Mrs. Webster to look up the articles. He would have to reserve judgment until he knew more.

He would wait. Too many people had done too much in recent weeks. It was almost always better to do nothing.

Peter had not looked well recently. He had looked as though he had not been sleeping. There had been something cadaverish about him, and he had never been exactly plump to begin with.

And hadn't there, now that he thought about it, been a scratch on one of his arms? Peter had fingered it during a meeting. A cut, not at all well healed, much like the claw mark a cat might make.

But Langton knew nothing of Peter's sexual habits. Didn't like to give it a thought. There were torrid affairs in which a man might be scratched a bit. Langton remembered a night or two himself in which pleasure and pain had been confused. That was the way with passion. He was not a scientist, but he kept a broad view of things.

On his wrist. A claw mark.

Harry worked his nose into the grass around a white post.

If only Higg were back from near-death. Langton needed help. He was not made for this sort of crisis. What would Higg suggest? Something active. "We ought to go on down to his flat this very night and see what sort of mischief he's up to." Or, at the very least, "Talk to that man the first thing tomorrow morning. You know there's something wrong." But Higg would be so much better at confronting possible madmen than Langton would ever be.

Now Langton had indigestion. He would chew three or four Setter's and try to find something to read. Nothing with a crime in it, or a mystery.

He tugged Harry along the pavement. The entire chain of mishaps might have been Peter's doing. He certainly knew enough about machinery to cause a generator to blow up. It was not impossible that he had stolen the Skeldergate Man and sold him to the international market. One or two items of the Sutton Hoo exhibit had vanished a few years ago, he had heard, and only luck turned them up in a drug raid in Paris. There was always a potential for crime in archaeology. A dig could be salted with treasures in order to inflate its importance to the press, or to the foundation funding the dig. Finds could disappear. Langton had a good deal of experience, and everyone he knew had been honest and diligent.

Peter had seemed hardworking, and, ignoring his past, entirely respectable. But there was something wrong with Peter now, and Langton had, suddenly, too many questions to wait until morning.

But he had to wait. He couldn't go knocking people up at three or four in the morning to make wild accusations.

He couldn't, but Davis could. Davis would be pleased to do something—anything—to recover the missing bog man. He was the sort of man who loved action. Langton would ask for Davis's help before he confronted Peter. That was the way to handle it—no need to run a risk by taking on too much by himself.

Langton returned to his home, and sat trying to read a historical novel he had enjoyed years before. Unfortunately, the novel took place in Anglo-Saxon times, and this reminded him of the Skeldergate dig.

His wife tottered forth and asked him if he were coming to bed at all that night, or sitting up like a silly owl.

"Like an owl," he said.

"How many more years of this will we go through, Charles?" she asked.

The question of retirement. She had aired this before, and he still did not know. He did not have to speak. She read his face, his posture.

She amazed him. Dishes and pots had flown across the kitchen, shattering like crockery in a hurricane, and yet now she was more than calm—sleepy. Sometimes women seemed wiser and stronger than men. She was a deep and lovely mystery.

"You'll wear yourself out," she said.

He did not have to respond. She left him sitting alone.

Langton read, and watched the clock, praying that night would pass quickly.

163

26

Irene did not like the way the train rolled through the dark. It was fast enough for an ordinary journey, but not fast enough for this night.

The reason for her sudden trip was very simple: she understood what was happening. She had been walking across Russell Square, on the way to the Bloomsbury flat she shared with an old girlfriend, when she understood everything.

Peter is dangerous. He is too sick. Something must be done or a terrible thing will happen. She had understood, hurrying across the square in a sudden current of cold, what Peter had done.

She had not bothered to return to the flat, but had flagged a cab. She had a return ticket, so she was able to run and catch a train just as it was about to leave. She had been foolish not to see it before. And now so much depended on her. And on the speed of the train. There were delays, and a voice droned over the metal roar of the rails announcing a delay at Doncaster.

She clenched her fists. If the train was slow, rattling through the night, then she could do nothing.

She had not bothered to telephone Davis. Let him be surprised. Besides, she understood things that Davis was not yet ready to accept. She had always preferred to be independent. She would take care of everything. She wanted to hold Davis, and felt her hands tremble at the thought. She wanted to stitch a message through the darkness, across the blank, empty fields: Oh, Davis. Be careful. Be very careful.

Davis, she thought: Be safe. I am on my way.

Peter was a sick man, and sick men make mistakes. Irene nearly smiled, despite her icy hands, her icy feet. She would stop him herself.

It had gone magnificently. Better than he had dared to dream.

He folded his costume, and put it on the back seat, beside his passenger. They were all leaving. There was no reason to stay here any longer. He shut the door as quietly as possible. The Austin started, and he eased it into gear.

Peter forced himself to drive slowly. He crossed the Lendal Bridge, not shifting out of second. There was no traffic, and there were no police, as far as he could see, but he did not want to do anything wrong at this point.

"I don't want to make a mistake now," he said to his passenger, who lay, as though drowsing, on the back seat.

"Don't want any mistakes at this point," he continued, "after everything has gone so well."

More than well. Perfectly.

He leaped from the car, and unlocked the gate. He shot the car through the narrow gap. This would not take very long at all.

It was a blessing. The chorus of voices in his head had stopped. The little sounds around him were clear again. The rasp of his work boot on the earth, the tinkle of the keys.

The dig was a well of darkness. It would be easy to make a mistake of another sort here, he thought, and fall into one of the trenches. Best be careful. Best be very careful.

And fast. The thing to do now was to flee. Get his few things together, his notebooks—mustn't let them see any of those. He might have scribbled something in a book that might tell them everything. He had made notes. He had used scissors from his desk to cut the burlap. Even a thread of cloth would betray him. Just a few minutes to clean his desk, and then he would be gone.

He did not know where, but there was no reason to expect that his genius would fail him now. He had a great talent. He was one of the most brilliant men in the world, and he did not have to worry about anything.

And the Man would be worth something. Wouldn't there be private collectors somewhere in the world who would crave such a possession? Necessarily secret, of course, but entirely unique. Switzerland, no doubt, with the Man folded easily like the leather handbag he very nearly was. He would be easy to hide. And no one would guess that Peter had done this. He would leave a note. "Professional pressures too great. Need a few days away."

He parked the car as close to the office as he could. The ground was uneven, scarred with ruts, and pocked with puddles.

When the car's motor was switched off everything was quiet. His own breath was loud. "Yes," he told himself. "I taught him a very good lesson. A well-deserved lesson. A very important lesson that he will never forget."

How foolish people were! An intelligent man like Davis believed that a bog man could walk. Now Davis was probably dead. Peter certainly hoped so. Dead, his last moments hideous.

Peter laughed and laughed until the small car shook.

The most wonderful, most delightful joke anyone had ever played, and it was a pity Davis would never know what a tremendous joke it was. Peter wiped a tear. It was simply all too wonderful.

Every step had been brilliant. The night he stole the Man, for example—wrapping the Man's hand around the door handle for a moment had been a choice bit. That had no doubt pleased them no end. The police must be very happy indeed to think they were tracking a twelve-hundred-year-old fugitive.

If only he could tell the tale, thought Peter. How impressed everyone would be.

He unlocked the office Portakabin, and shut the door behind him quietly. Every sound seemed so loud. His breath seemed to roar. He switched on an electric torch, and turned the torch toward the wall. No one could see him here. He would be quick, and quiet. He tugged open his desk drawer.

Yes, here was a sketch, in this W. H. Smith notebook. The frame was drawn in pencil, the frame that even now gave the Man his structure. Peter tucked the notebook into his pocket. God only knew whatever else he had scrawled. He had been confused, even feverish, for quite some time.

But all that was over. Now he was going to be calm, and very careful.

He froze, and held his breath. A sound. A click, or a snap. A lock, perhaps. He listened, and heard only his own heartbeat thud like a machine. A heart made an ugly thump if you really listened to it, didn't it? Ugly, and loud, as well.

Then there had been the terrible thing that had happened, the thing that Peter groaned to think about. He would weep if he let himself remember it. He would weep, and be unable to sort this drawer.

He had too many notes. Computer printouts, scraps of paper. It was a good idea to clean this desk—he found a design, scribbled on a finds card, of the knee hinge. If you knew what it was, the secret was made clear. Otherwise, it looked like a bit of sloppy Leonardo. Clever, but enigmatic. He could take no risks. Keep it all perfect, he told himself. Leave them blind.

There was too much here. The best way to make sure he left nothing behind was to burn it all. He had what he needed, a box of matches. A fire would attract attention, though, and this was what he wanted to avoid.

He was weeping despite himself. It had been too terrible.

Jane had come into his flat, using a key he had given her long ago, and she had written him a note.

A kind note, affectionate. Not loving, but a note he would have treasured if he had not been forced to tear it into bits and flush it down the toilet.

He had found her dead in his flat. How she had died was a mystery, but the closet had been open. She must have looked into it and seen the Man, and died of shock. This was hard to understand, but he had found the Man lying next to her, as though she had taken it out of the closet and intended to take it with her, and then suffered a failure, quite literally, of heart.

A brutal discovery. The sorrow had made him tear furniture to bits, the blond pine table, and the two benches. He had torn them apart out of grief. Even now, hot tears kissed his hands as he worked.

Jane.

It had made him all the more determined that Davis suffer. He hoped Davis was lying even now with his face smashed in, teeth and pulp down his throat.

167

He wept. Gradually he gathered his thoughts, and breathed more easily.

He had committed her to the river. He could not run the risk of having the Man discovered, not while the intelligence breathed into his ear, not while everything was going so well.

But it had given him a bad thought, a thought that flowered in him even now: Maybe there was something to it. Perhaps—although it was impossible—perhaps the Man *was* able to move by himself. Something had nearly killed Dr. Higg, and certainly Jane was dead.

Peter forced himself to laugh. See how nervous he had become! He was as foolish as any of them, nearly as nerve-shattered as Davis.

But there was a sound. A real sound. He could not move as the door opened behind him with a dry, empty laugh of its hinges.

A voice said, "I hope I am in time, Peter."

Peter did not pause to wonder, or to formulate a response. He turned, saw who it was, and knew immediately that he would have to kill her.

Irene's eyes were bright. "I hurried back from London, and then I thought, I wonder if he is at the site. You see how well I am beginning to understand you, Peter. I saw the lights, and now I see you standing there, looking unwell."

She was panting slightly, carrying only a handbag. She put it down and unzipped her jacket, as though she were someone arriving for a long-planned meeting.

Peter's voice was a rasp. "I am up late," he began. "And so are you."

"I have come all the way from London tonight for a reason, Peter."

Peter had begun to believe himself entirely brilliant again. He would be able to talk her out of whatever she thought. And yet there was something about Irene that made her indomitable. Her eyes were too bright, and she seemed always to be about to smile, as though she knew, always, too much.

"I have work," Peter offered, panting, unable to control his breathing. "Catching up to do."

"I believe, Peter, that you stole the Skeldergate Man, and took our poor old friend away and hid him."

He stared, and then he experimented with a smile. "Why would I do that?"

"I believe that you have been taking advantage of the rumors here, Peter. The stories about the site, and how it is haunted. You want to scare us, I don't know why. I think perhaps you dislike someone among us, perhaps Davis. Perhaps you want to frighten him, or frighten all of us. But I understand other things, too, Peter."

Kill her. The command was like a slap. Kill her now. A snarl from within his bones.

"I think perhaps you have underestimated the site, and our old friend the bog man. Perhaps you are the one who has been deceived, Peter. Perhaps the spirit of this place has possessed you and used you to give our old friend a new life. Perhaps the Man is using you, Peter, and perhaps you should be warned."

She said this lightly, as though disagreeing on the accuracy of a train schedule. But her eyes were steady. Peter could not answer her, and in his hesitation she saw that she was right.

"I am so glad I came here, Peter. Because I know it is true. You have done something terrible. Have you—I cannot even ask it. Have you hurt Davis?"

Peter turned and mentally discarded the objects he saw. Even the scissors looked difficult, undependable, and he needed something sure. Something like a mattock, or a hammer, or—he saw it.

The Bulldog spade was in his hand.

Irene told him everything with her eyes: that she saw how late she was, how truly too late. And she was determined that it would be difficult to kill her. She flung herself across the cabin to a chair, and lifted the chair to keep him away from her.

It did not even slow him down, this minor obstruction. His movements were fluid, and swifter than she could have imagined. He swung wide, and the spade rang with the sound of the blow.

But she did not go down. She speared him with a leg of the chair, and all the breath left his body. She lunged toward the door, and he caught her with one hand and managed to bounce her off the table, the kettle clattering.

She was on her feet at once, picking up the chair, and this time he planted his feet, and swung harder.

There was no moment of falling. One moment she was upright, fending him away with the chair. The next she was on the floor, and he tore the chair from her grasp. He struck her again, but the unconscious rolling of her head made the blow half miss, and the spade handle splintered.

Peter fell to his knees. He was sweating, and his arms trembled. He could not even bring himself to laugh, aside from a croak.

Now he had a problem. Now he had a dead body, and this would not be so simple. He would have to put her somewhere quickly, somewhere no one would look for days, or, better, weeks. The river could not be trusted. Bodies tend to float. He could anchor the corpse, but as he considered this he realized exactly where he should put her.

He was barely trembling as he gathered her, and began to half carry, half drag her. He gathered up her handbag. He was not so foolish as to forget that. He would put her and her handbag in the discard heap, among the slag, the slabs of concrete, and the screened soil. She could stay there for months.

He was trembling now with delight. Even this disaster would be overcome. He found a place quickly, settling two or three chunks of concrete over her. It was too quick, he realized. He would need to find another spade and do the job as it should be done.

At the last moment, hurrying back to the cabin, he realized something about her body. As he had carried it he had felt it moving. Slightly. Just barely. He had felt it breathing.

She was still alive.

He clenched his fists. He could not deny it. He had not killed her.

He would fix that. He would clean his desk, find a new spade, and go back where she was, pinned under concrete. She would not go anywhere.

He sat at his desk. He could not stop shivering. What a mess this office was, he saw. Bits of spade handle. An overturned chair. And blood, bright spatters of it. He had a good deal of work to do, and he began, gathering wood bits, righting the chair, making the cabin look like a place of business.

A sound, somewhere out there in the darkness. It could not be Irene. There was no way that she could scramble out from under the concrete slag. And besides, it did not sound like a human being at all. There was a click, and then a long, whispering sound. It sounded like something dragging through the dark.

Surely there was nothing. Surely it was imaginary. But there was, he convinced himself, something. Something real. He crouched, tilting his head. He could not hear the sound now, but there had been a click again, metallic and sharp.

Someone was out there. Someone shuffled slowly in the dark. There was a step, and a drag, and another step. Someone with a limp, or a very irregular stride. A drunk man, perhaps. That is exactly how it sounded. A drunk man out there, staggering through the dark.

Coming closer.

There was a shape at the window. It was infuriating how disrespectful drink made people. Nosy and obnoxious. Dark hands worked at the window frame. The man was trying to break into the office. Peter clenched his teeth. It was a very good thing he was here to prevent what was, quite plainly, a crime about to take place.

He parted his lips to warn the man away, and then he had a much more brilliant idea. He would let the crime begin, and he would surprise the would-be burglar in his tracks.

Peter took a sharp breath. There was something wrong.

It was not a burglar.

It was not a man.

The dark hands patted at the glass, and then retreated. The shuffling step carried itself along the outside of the cabin. A foot found, and missed, and found again the bottom step.

The Skeldergate Man was climbing the steps. His hands pattered on the outside of the door, feeling it, by the whispering sounds they made, like slow black butterflies.

Peter felt his life stop, and believed that he would never move again. His heart clattered in his chest, and in his ears. The Man— the leathery thing that had been a man—had begun to walk on its own.

It made no sound but the pad of its hands on the outside of the door. No sound at all.

This was impossible, entirely impossible, and he should simply stride to the door, and open it, and stuff the tiresome corpse back into the car where it belonged. This was funny in its way, wasn't it? A fine invention, one that wouldn't shut off.

The door handle began to move. Shakily, but relentlessly, it twisted from horizontal to vertical. This was impossible as well, Peter thought to himself, feeling his mind become paralyzed. The hand had no strength in it at all for a very good reason. It had no bones. It could not turn a door handle.

The door opened. The silhouette was a darker shape against the less perfect dark of night.

Peter backed away, all the way to the computer. He would go out to the car and get the controls, as soon as he could move again.

The corpse stood upright, trembling slightly, swinging its head from side to side, a blind thing. It lurched into the cabin, and Peter dashed past it, down the steps.

It was a very good thing to be out under the sky. The cabin had been a trap. Now that he was out, he knew how easy it would be to resolve this crisis. He would run. It was very simple. And at the same time he found Irene's words burning into him.

The Man had been using him.

He turned toward the car. He would lock himself in there, and he would have a chance to think. That's all he needed. A moment to think. Just a moment to understand what was happening. But he was puzzled.

There was something around his neck. Nothing terribly strong. Something snakelike, and constricting. It tightened, and there was a weight behind it, dragging along the ground.

He spun, tangled in this obstruction, and for some reason he could not see clearly. It was dark, he knew, but he could not understand why his vision was so obscured.

There was a head in the way, just before his eyes, and the bindings that held him, and grew tighter, were leathery straps, the arms and legs of the Man.

Peter wrestled, and worked his way out of the leather lashes that held him, but which were, after all, quite light. He was very deeply puzzled as to how he had become entangled in them. He must have brushed the Man as he leaped past, toward the door. As he tried to strip himself of the ancient leather, one arm worked itself up toward Peter's face.

Toward his mouth. Peter cringed, backing away, but the thing would not leave him.

The hand found his lips. Leather fingers forced themselves between his teeth. Peter bit hard, trying to cry out, because this was not the powerless, device-driven thing he had known. This thing was alive. A wind, like ancient breath, icy as the exhalation of a cave, kissed Peter's cheeks. The taste of the ancient hand was tannic, like a new glove, and the leather limb forced its way into Peter's throat, and down. Peter gagged, his scream silenced. The face touched Peter's face, and Peter danced, struggling to toss the thing away.

172

The hand reached into Peter, and made a fist inside him. He could feel it like a knot as he danced, and he leaped and spun and ran, until he knew that he could not breathe, and had not been able to breathe for a long time.

Peter rolled on the ground, hammering the skull before him with his own. He tore at the thing, unable to hang on to it, and when he did find the throat before him, the neck collapsed easily within his grip.

The hand within Peter worked, spasming, searching. Peter fell, stood again, fought, fell, and rolled.

He rolled into a place that was not earth, but was an opening, and he fell, his mouth stretched in an unutterable scream.

27

It was sleep. Not good sleep—something was wrong. But no dreams. He turned his head, and a stone in his skull rolled and careened.

He took a breath, and it hurt. He was wet. He tasted hot salt water. He would be fine if he did not move. No moving. No moving at all.

Must live. The thought shook him. He might be dying, he realized, and he began to climb upward, out of the wet place that floated him.

Concrete at his cheek. He blinked. A brick wall.

It all came back. How long ago had it been? he asked himself. Not long. A light was on, and another. A head looked out to see what was happening, and Davis would have called but all the words had been slammed out of him.

He had landed with an impact greater than anything he had ever known. Like a great balloon bursting, but he had been the balloon.

Dead now, he thought. Now I'm dead.

Not dead. It was impossible to believe, but the evidence was there. Only a minute or two had passed since he fell. No time at all.

Not hours. Otherwise, why was someone still looking out to see what the noise had been?

Davis mouthed the words he had no strength to speak. Down here. Here. I'm here.

I fell.

The two lights went off.

He must have slept again. Perhaps he had tried to move too quickly. He woke again, with a nausea that came and went, like a flashing light.

He tried to judge the time. It was, he thought, much closer to morning. The world seemed hushed, and the sky too dark. A bird squeaked somewhere, a voice from another world.

If he slept again he would not wake.

He would save himself. That would be easy, if he could walk. He wondered if that would be possible.

He would move his body. That was a very good plan. Davis had always liked plans. Formulate a plan, and carry it out.

Move the body. Shock. He would go into shock, and he would die of that, now that he had survived everything else. The thought angered him, and he moved his arms. He was wearing a shirt. And pants. He had not undressed before lying down. Yes, it all came back to him.

He worked his legs. Arms and legs. Good. Very important. He shakily felt himself, his chest, which was wet and warm, and, with great hesitation, his upper thighs, and the seat of his pants, which were wet, but not, he could tell, with great relief, impaled on a spear fence. His crotch felt intact. He was sprawled on cold concrete, and it was not such a bad place to rest.

Then he remembered all of it.

The Skeldergate Man.

His sightless eyes. His leathery, empty arms.

He had to warn people. He had to tell everyone.

But now Davis was afraid. He was very cold, and he did not have the strength to shiver. The cold rose from his toes, up his legs, into his torso. Shock from his injuries, he told himself, and fear.

Shuddering, Davis dragged himself to the brick wall. His legs danced with spasms. He investigated his ankles with his hands. He winced. He had, apparently, landed on his feet, half crouched. This had been his plan. The merest touch hurt, but he did not think they were broken. Hanging onto the drain had slowed his fall just enough.

Something wrong with my ribs, too, he thought. And my skull. But the damage did not seem mortal. There was a flutter of joy. He was alive, and he would be strong again some day.

This sense of great happiness gave him a strange detachment from his fear, and he understood what had happened. It was funny, although he could not laugh. It was amazingly funny. The greatest joke ever played on anyone.

A brilliant joke.

Peter was a genius, and he was also very sick.

Davis clawed the brick wall, struggling to stand. It was a risk. If his ankles were sprained he would sprawl again. He leaned, sweating icily, and let the brick wall support him for a long time. He did not really have to move again for a long time.

Not for a long, long time.

Peter was mad.

Must move now. Must try to take a step.

The slashed thighs crippled him, and his ankles barely supported his weight. He staggered. The blood on his shirt was from his mouth, he discovered, exploring with his fingers. He had bit his lips badly. He did not seem to be missing any teeth.

The next part would be difficult. The back steps. But they weren't so hard. The back door was difficult, because it was locked. He would not have the strength to stagger around the row of buildings, to the front door to begin ringing flats, trying to wake someone to come down and haul him up.

He had the strength. Swaying, he crept around the building, climbed from spear to spear along the black rail fence, and dragged himself up the front steps.

He was gathering himself to begin pushing the buttons to all the flats, when a familiar figure hurried up the street in the dawn.

Davis grinned, and tried to wave.

Mr. Langton scurried toward the front steps, still not seeing what awaited him.

"Don't worry, Mr. Langton," said Davis. "It's not as bad as it looks."

Langton faltered and gasped. He fell to one knee and tried to drag himself to his feet, one hand on the rail.

"I'm all right, Mr. Langton," said Davis. "Just a little bit banged up."

Langton opened his mouth and shut it. "Davis," he whispered. "Is that you?"

"I fell."

"What has he done to you?"

That, Davis thought, will take some telling.

"We must get you to a doctor. Can you stand?"

Davis stood, hunched, and bleeding again, but on his feet. "I want you to listen to me," Davis began, enunciating as clearly as he could with his puffy lips. "We have to hurry."

"Indeed we will." Langton began pushing bells to the flats. "Is there a telephone in this building?"

"Listen to me."

"I'm responsible for this. I should have known that Peter was far more sick than we all thought. I was swept along by all the optimism."

"Langton, shut up and listen to me."

"Optimism is a half step ahead of foolhardiness."

No one answered. Of course not, Davis thought. The missing Mandy was in the ground-floor flat, a furtive woman who was never home was, as usual, absent from the cellar flat, Peter was gone, and Davis was here on the steps. He tried to enumerate the flats on his fingers. There were one or two others he could not think of just now.

"This," said Davis, "is what we will do."

28

Davis opened the door of Langton's Ford, and dragged himself from the car. He tucked the crutches under one arm and hobbled along without them. The pain was bad, but he ignored it as well as he could.

The dig was exposed in the midmorning light, trenches and scaffolding which should have been a hive of scientific activity all silent and still.

Peter's Austin was parked beside the main cabin. The rear door was open. Davis lifted a hand to close it, but stopped himself.

Peter was here. Somewhere on the site. He would not leave his car like this, one door open. He was here, at this moment, watching them.

There were many places to hide. Various cabins and sheds, and, if he did not mind wallowing in groundwater, various trenches.

"Entirely foolish business," said Langton.

Davis lifted a finger to his lips. It was not an easy gesture, as stiff as he was. "He's here."

"Here?"

"I think he can hear us," he whispered.

Langton stiffened. "I should have brought Harry, my dog. Harry would root him out, however he tried to hide."

They hesitated at the main office. The door was open. Davis was extremely puzzled. There was something very odd about all of this. Had they interrupted Peter just now? Peter would have fled hours ago, Davis thought. There was no reason for him to lurk around the dig.

"If he can hear us, he may as well know what we think of him," said Langton. There was not much confidence in his voice. If Peter was here, as sick as he was, this was a very dangerous place to be.

The office was the same as always, casually disorganized. There were spoons scattered on the floor, and a patch of what looked like beet juice.

But it was messier than usual, Davis realized. There was a white splinter of wood, and the stump of a spade leaning in the corner. That patch on the floor was not beet juice.

Davis could not have guessed why, but the first call he made was to Irene's flat here in York. He had no reason to expect her to be there, and yet his fingers made the decision for him. There was no answer.

Langton began heating some water. Langton was swept with disgust for himself and fury toward Peter. The sort of very sick mind that could invent a contrivance like that, as a cruel and repulsive joke, was a fit enemy for any man. Langton would not rest until Peter had paid some sort of ultimate price for this. It was unforgivable.

Langton was extremely uncertain regarding Davis's health. He was no doubt quite ill, and should be in hospital resting. The casualty physician had been appalled. "Surely you don't intend to leave," he had said. Langton had found Davis's answer quite appropriate. "If a twelve-hundred-year-old man can walk around, then I can, too." The doctor had been baffled, but Langton had, reluctantly, agreed.

"We're a tough lot," Langton had said. "Archaeologists, you know. Always taking a fall over one thing or another." Langton was thankful to share this burden with someone. Langton knew his own qualities. He was an excellent second-in-command, and a master at worrying over details. He had to admit, grudgingly, that Davis had a certain amount of character. The time for doing nothing was quite plainly past. This day would require decisiveness. Davis was a decisive man.

Davis put down the telephone, but at once picked it up again. Irene was not in her London flat. Her roommate, a soft-voiced young woman, said that Irene had not spent the night there. Davis was grateful to the cheerful and courteous information operators who found the magazine she worked for.

Miss Saarni was not at her desk.

"This is extremely urgent."

"One moment, please."

The phone line made fine, dry whispers, the electronic equivalent of silence.

No, Miss Saarni was not there. No one knew where she might be.

Langton stirred coffee. "Sugar?"

"Absolutely. Sugar and codeine. The working man's breakfast."

"Any time you feel the need to lie down, Davis—"

"No need for that. I feel terrific."

He was sitting at Peter's desk. The drawer had not been shut all the way. It could not be shut, he realized. It was a jumble of computer printouts and W. H. Smith spiral notebooks. It looked as though Peter had been ransacking his own desk, looking for something. Something had interrupted him.

"Don't you feel," Davis began. "That there is something very strange?"

"Quite."

"I mean—here. Something not right."

Danger, thought Davis. He dragged himself to his feet. But not simply danger. He stood at the doorway, surveying the dig. There was something wrong. It was right before him, within view, and he could not tell what it was.

The Austin, with its back door open. The Ford. The trenches.

The blood on the floor. "I can't sit here like this. There's something wrong."

"There's no reason to worry over Irene, Davis. She might have made other plans."

A burly figure strode through the gate, and closed it behind him. The man waved.

"Skip!" cried Davis.

"Our old friend Skip!" cried Langton, because if anyone could defend them from a madman it was this stout man.

"I was glad to hear from you, Mr. Langton. I was thinking of all of you, all night. I kept wondering when we would start in again. But the others aren't here yet?" he asked, rubbing his hands together, in that half-question, half-statement Yorkshire lilt.

"We only wanted you," said Davis. "A good deal has happened."

Skip stroked his beard and sipped coffee while Davis spoke.

"All this is true?" he said at last. "What really happened?"

"All true," said Davis.

"There's no end to what a sick mind might do," said Langton.

Davis was not sure how to ask. "Have you, Skip, noticed anything strange about the dig?"

"Unusual, like?"

"There's something wrong here, and I can't think what it is."

"That's easy. Trench Five has fallen in again."

Davis went cold.

"I noticed it on my way in. It's as bad as the time it tried to kill Oliver and myself," said Skip, finishing his coffee.

Davis took a lurching step. He did not like this. "Get a shovel," he said softly.

Skip dug. He did not bother to empty the dirt into buckets. Quickly but carefully, he flung earth. One shallow scoop after another was tossed aside. It took skill, unpeeling just enough earth, and continuing, working lightly, but so quickly that earth quickly piled into a peak behind him.

At last he stopped. He turned to look up at Davis. "Something here, all right," he said.

"Keep going," said Davis. His mouth was dry. The worst possible thing had happened. Langton and Skip thought they had a battle with a madman on their hands. Davis knew better.

"There's something like an arm," said Skip.

Mud the shape of a hand thrust itself from the earth. Davis prayed. There was still hope. Still a speck of hope. As Skip worked, the hand seemed to sculpt into an arm but it was still earth-black.

Skip used a brush. The mud was whisked free, and the true color of the hand was exposed.

It was pale.

Skip dragged Peter's body from the earth.

"We shouldn't move it," said Langton.

Skip brushed mud from the slack face.

"I'll call the police," said Langton, when he could speak.

Davis's grip on his arm stopped him. "What we do is this. Listen to me, Langton—you must do as I say."

"I'm too tired to put up with anything like hysterics, Davis."

"I don't think you understand what's happening. We must protect all of us, all of the living, from the fury of the dead." He stopped himself. The phrase had surprised him, even as he had uttered it.

Skip was standing in the middle of the site. He had dropped the mattock, and was examining something in his hands, a small object that glittered.

"Lipstick," he called.

Davis joined him.

"Never used," said Skip.

Davis thought, at once, that Irene never used makeup, and that it was just like her to buy it and then forget that she had it in her handbag.

As he thought this he realized that there was no doubt in his mind. This had fallen out of Irene's handbag, and so had this. He knelt to pluck a green and orange British Rail ticket from a puddle. The milk-and-coffee-colored water had stained it, but he could read it easily. It was a return ticket from London to York. He could feel the crescent-shaped puncture hole where the ticket had been canceled.

"Irene is here," he said, half to himself. Then he turned and called, "She's here!"

Both men stared a question.

"Irene is here!"

It did not take them long to find her resting place. Concrete slabs had been tipped to one side, and there was blood where her head had been, a small black spill of it.

But Irene was gone.

Davis sat in the Portakabin while the police searched, questioned, made notes, spoke into the little black radios they wore on their collars, and asked Davis three different times for a description of the missing woman, and three different times asked him what, exactly, was the relationship between Davis and Miss Saarni.

They questioned Skip on the discovery of Peter's body. The

attitude of the police was dumbfounded displeasure. Langton was crisp with them. No one had any idea what had happened, what was happening, or what would happen. They recognized in him a man who knew how to write a potent letter of complaint, and so they left, at last, with something like a courteous farewell and a promise to get results.

Davis smoldered, waiting for the last policeman to leave. Irene was gone. And yet he could feel it in his bones—she was not far away. These police, he thought, with their officious searching and blood sampling and all their questions, would never find her. Perhaps they did not even believe that it was Irene who was missing. She would turn up, they might think, with a hangover in some hotel somewhere, with a good friend she had not gotten around to mentioning yet.

"Now that they've gone," said Davis, finally, "we can start looking."

He hobbled out, and gazed at the trenches. She could be anywhere. Here on the site. In the river. Gone completely.

Skip had gone off to the Petergate Fishery for a late lunch which he alone felt like eating. Langton paced the cabin, squinted at the sky, called his wife, and at last said, watching Davis limp among the scaffolding and wheelbarrows, "There's no use looking, Davis. The police gave things a good look-round, you know."

What are we, thought Davis, if not people who, by professional inclination and training, find the lost, the buried?

"What do you suppose, Davis?" called Langton. "That she's gone down a hole somewhere?"

And then Davis saw it.

183

29

Irene felt the pain turning, a sheet that blew in the wind, sometimes reflecting angry light, and sometimes softness, shadow. If she moved, she knew, she would die of pain. So, she reasoned to herself, I will not move, for a very long time.

But she could not help wondering where she was. Where she was, and why she was wet. It could not be blood, she told herself. It is too cold for blood. I must, she decided, open my eyes, and look.

Perhaps she slept. When she woke again, she found herself with her eyes opening, and seeing light glitter off a wall. It was a stone wall, and moss was green in the crack of light. She was underground. There was a beautiful sound, like the chattering of budgies. It was, she decided, the musical tinkle of water.

So now I am in a very strange place, she thought. And how did I get here, alone? She stretched an arm to touch the wall, and then her arm shrank back.

She was not alone. There was someone here. But there was something very wrong. So wrong she could not think it for a moment.

There was a body there, just beyond her head. But the body

was not breathing. Then, she told herself, if the body is not breathing, it is dead.

The body moved. It was the whisper of leather, the hiss of coarse weave being drawn with the movement, the sound, too, somewhere muffled, of metal rotating, clicking into place. As though the person with her had a metal skeleton.

But it was breathing, she told herself. Listen to it. Long, slow breaths, perhaps one every minute, more like something pretending to breathe than a human being sustaining himself on air. Breathing because it remembered that is what the living do.

Irene was almost never afraid. There was simply no use, she knew, in being afraid now. She sat up suddenly. There was bright, savage pain, and then something worse.

A snakelike arm wrapped around her neck, and squeezed her until she could not breathe. She felt the fury of this Man, this ancient fury that would not let her go. She struggled with both hands, and then felt the strength bleed from her body.

The arm was a leather cord around her neck. This was how she would die, she thought, wrestling with the being she could not see, falling back onto the wet earth.

The arm let her go. He does not want me dead, she thought. He wants my warmth. He wants to keep me alive and near him, as a man might keep a fire burning. He only needs my warmth.

But she was up again, calling Davis's name, struggling to be free of this leather blanket, this living, slithering leather frame that engulfed her, and covered her mouth with its hands.

She could not move. Her pain and the Man's embrace knotted her. It was a long struggle, and with every movement the leather embrace tightened.

It was then that she thought she heard it. How amusing the mind could be. Even then she appreciated the humor of it. She thought she heard Davis call her name. Just once. It was exactly like his voice, wondering, earnest, doubtful. Would this be her last thought? Imagining that she heard the sound of Davis's voice?

Only when she felt the leather hands touch her skin again, and not only the skin of her face, but the skin under her blouse, feeling her, needing the warmth of her body, did she begin to scream.

185

30

It was in one of the neglected trenches, long ago measured, scraped, screened, and photographed. It was a trench where work had not been taking place, he supposed, since the beginning of the dig. That was how he spotted it: the new crack in the side of the trench, down where the groundwater was deepest.

Davis would not have noticed it if he had not made himself familiar with the site long before this. It was hardly remarkable that the police had missed it. It was a slight fissure in the earth, nothing more.

Davis crept down the steps, and nearly slipped when he reached the bottom. This was all cold muck, and he doubted, now that he examined the fissure, that it was anything but a subsidence, a slippage. It was nothing of any special interest.

And yet he stayed where he was. Some of the Etruscan tombs, when they were discovered, looked like this. Some of them were found when a plow broke through the field, through the roof of a tomb, into ancient treasure.

He crept even closer to the fissure, and peered in. There was something here, after all. He could feel the cold of a great inner chamber, a cavern. There was a tinkle of groundwater somewhere far within.

It was a vault, the remains, he imagined, of an ancient fortress tower, perhaps the bottom story of a bastion. Once it had stood beside the river. Now it was underground, a reservoir.

On another day, in another place, this would have been an exciting discovery. He was about to climb to his feet, when he stopped himself. He took a sharp breath and tilted his head.

Surely he was imagining things, but it sounded as though someone inside this darkness had just whispered his name. He had heard it, but he had also not-heard it—hoping for it.

Because there was nothing here but emptiness. The cold exhalation from the earth kept Davis where he was, kneeling and wishing his cuts did not throb. His own pain did not interest him, really. It was the thought of Irene that burned in him.

This opening was large enough—a man could squeeze through it, and yet this was not the time for exploration. If only there were any real sound from inside, any evidence that Irene was here.

Kneeling there, listening, he heard nothing that sounded human. No sound that indicated that this was where Irene was hidden. It was an empty chamber—a scientific discovery, one that would have astounded him on any other day, but which today meant only that Irene was still lost.

He called her name, knowing as he did it that he was calling to empty dark, empty earth. The answer was silence, worse than silence—the absence of any answer at all. It was a cry into a void.

He dragged himself to his feet, and slogged through the brown water. As his hands gripped the cold steel of the ladder he heard it.

But surely not. It was impossible. He made himself listen harder, and then he was certain. It was a scream. It was Irene. It was Irene, trapped somewhere in the chamber, within the earth.

Davis dived toward the crack, and fought the wet clay, gasping, jackknifing his body. He had been wrong—the fissure was not wide enough for a man. Indeed, it seemed to be closing on him.

And then he was within, sprawling on a mud-slick stone floor. The music of the splashing water was louder, and the dark was nearly perfect.

He called her name.

"It is dangerous here, Davis," said Irene somewhere in the

dark. The sound of her voice ignited a feeling of joy that was nearly pain. Then something kept her from speaking, muffling her.

Davis fought himself upright, and it was as though a whip lashed his neck. A leather strap wrapped around his throat, and a leg snaked its way between his, and Davis fell.

He fell hard, and for a moment could not move his arms. When he could command his hands, he could not seize an opponent who seemed to be all shapes at once. His eyes could not make out his opponent's face, but Davis did not have to see. He knew. It was one of those moments when the mind, in great danger, is lucid enough to survey the truth.

What he fought was fury, a fury beyond imagining. This dead man would not forgive the living for his unjust death. And even as Davis felt the breath squeezed from his body he realized how another member of the dead must hate him.

And for a moment Davis had an ugly thought: I deserve to die. For neglecting Margaret, I deserve this.

Then Irene's voice woke him. He seized the boneless head, but it was an octopus he was fighting, a thing with no shape and tremendous strength, with a flexible, whipping skeleton, that empowered this wrath.

The wrath was just, and yet as Davis rolled in the cold stone he felt the wrongfulness of his own death. He cried out. "No!"

He was stunned at his own anger, the fury of a living man. "It's wrong! You can't do this!"

She was beside them. "We do not seek to harm you, King Sigan. Please forgive your subjects," Irene was saying, in her musical voice.

Davis could barely whisper, "We want to honor you." The leather tightened. "King!" Davis choked the Anglo-Saxon: "Kyning Sigan!"

Still, the leather tightened. Centuries of vengeance made Davis's ribs creak. The leather lips were at Davis's own, and there was a sound from them, a groan, as of effort or a breathy curse.

Feeling flowed from Davis's body. Soon, Davis knew, he would have no thoughts, no fears—he would be gone. Already his legs and arms were numb.

"Your son is dead!" said Davis. "The people who killed you are dead!"

King Sigan's answer was to thrust his boneless arm down

Davis's throat. The dead king was twisting and working his hand to seize the lungs, smother the heart—to uproot a living man. Davis felt himself wither, his consciousness destroyed. Strength was nothing against this Being, the angry dead.

Irene was beside them both. Davis could sense her in the darkness, and sense her voice as she said, "Forgive us, King Sigan. We want to honor you."

Davis knew only that he would not die. He squeezed the soft skull of his adversary, and dragged the leather from his throat, pulling himself back to life with the knowledge that the dead, no matter how just their anger, did not have the right to destroy the living.

And he felt the ancient king falter. As though with doubt. As though the king realized for a moment that Davis was a living man, a man in love. As though King Sigan remembered his life, and did not want to kill.

At first Davis did not understand what was happening. Something splashed, and there was the chunky thud of stone on stone. And there was an immediate crush, a cold wave that half covered all of them.

The wave was very cold, and very heavy. It was followed by others. Even the king seemed to sense it, and went stiff with something like fear.

"The walls!" cried Irene.

The walls of the chamber were collapsing, burying them alive.

31

The tide of cold earth broke over them, down upon them, and Davis took a last breath, and reached out his hand toward Irene. He struggled through the churning mud, toward the crack of light, and the fragment of light was closing as he swam toward it.

The ancient king writhed to escape, making a long, airy scream. Davis dragged him. A hand thrust toward them from the outside, from the day.

Davis gripped the hand, and turned to find Irene. But Irene was already there, struggling through the slit of daylight. Then there were two hands reaching back for him, one of them Irene's. The hands had him, had both of them, as Davis wrestled with the earth that closed around him.

The sky. Davis was blinking up at the sky that fell over him, wet, cold. Irene's face was there, and Langton's. Langton was panting, and his face was mud-starred. "You were gone so long," said Langton. "I came looking for you—"

The mist was heavy, so heavy that it was premature night. Stone and mud continued to fall, churning, within the chamber until the crack was a bare scar on the surface and the empty chamber was a welter of rubble.

The king flexed, and Davis wrapped him in his arms. Langton's eyes were wide, and he backed away, splashing through the water.

"I need a sheet of plastic or canvas—whatever we have," called Davis. "And rope."

Irene was gone, too, and Davis was alone with his adversary. The leather body spasmed, but Davis held him from behind. The arms lashed the mist, and the legs worked to wrap around Davis, but Davis gripped the body hard and promised the king that all would be well.

"We'll find peace for you," said Davis.

For all of us.

The great vault of the Minster's nave arced high over them. It was night, and the ancient building was still. The only light came from beeswax candles. The flames were tiny, flickering cuts of cold, bare pinpricks at this distance.

It had to be dark, though. The Minster had to resemble a space that the king would recognize. Of course the medieval aspects of cathedral had been constructed long after this king's death. But it had been a cathedral in his day, and now it would be called upon to be an earlier, darker version of itself.

It was past midnight before Langton returned from London with the treasures they would need. The events of this day had given Langton a battered vigor. He was tired, but he had a warrior's enthusiasm for staying awake as long as possible. Dr. Higg's staff had raised an eyebrow or two. Langton had been his most peremptory. Let them wonder. Necessity was power.

Davis took the pack from Langton reverently, and did not speak for a moment. He was nearly afraid to look inside. What if Langton had brought the wrong treasures?

"They're all right," said Langton. "The circlet crown, and the enormous hilt. Go ahead and look."

Skip dug, his mattock rising and falling with a surprising lack of sound, beside the stones he had pried to get at earth. The eye adjusted to the dark, but the ear could not entirely adjust to the silence.

Skip plied his mattock, and at last climbed from the pit he had carved in the Minster floor.

The dirt was a small, dark mountain in a tarp. Skip gathered it together, and dragged it off. He used a broom, and then stood back to admire his work.

"Just like in medieval times, I'd say. You couldn't have much better than that."

"The question will be," said Davis, "will it look like a fit grave to an Anglo-Saxon king?"

"I thought you were sure of that," said Skip.

Davis shivered. "I wish I were."

Skip looked upward, at the roof he could not see in a darkness made magnificent by invisible architecture. "Let's find out."

There was the faintest scent of honey from the candles as they approached Irene, off in the darkest hollow of the nave, beside the wrapped, trussed body of the king. Irene knelt beside it, singing a soft, angular tune, her hand on the rolled tarp that imprisoned the body.

Davis nodded to Skip. The time had come.

Davis returned to the grave and rested the two treasures beside him, on the floor. But that was not right. That seemed disrespectful, somehow. He held them in his hands, and gazed down at them. He would cling to them, hoping for power from them. But there should be vestments and chanting. He hadn't even brought a Bible. They should have frankincense, and a priest.

Davis knew from Irene's cry that something was wrong. He turned, and a shape like a dark bird of prey skimmed through the dark, nearly flying across the stone floor, and was on Davis.

Davis grappled with the king, and worked the leather body to the floor. The shapeless skin gathered itself, but Davis stopped it with his hands, and with his thoughts.

The king knew. He knew what was about to happen, and he could hear what Davis was thinking, reading his prayers as he would have read written words.

We mourned you, said Davis in his mind, in his heart. We did not know what had happened. It is a terrible thing to be the living left behind. You do not know where the lost one has gone. You do not hear the step or the laugh.

Where do you go, now that you leave us, now that we go forward without you, into fortune and misfortune, and other loves, and age? Do not come to us, we cannot help you. It is you who help us, triumphant in your sleep. Look—what I have for you, honored, beloved dead.

They were in his hands, the circlet crown, and the sword hilt. For you, and for Margaret. These treasures, but more, our memories, and—our memories being so much of what we are—our lives. We bury them with you. Keep them for us, as you keep yourselves.

Davis sucked in a long, trembling breath. Warm blood trickled down the inside of his pant legs.

He gathered the king in his arms, and leaped down into the grave. He reached up to receive the treasures from Irene's hands. He thrust the hilt into the ancient hands. He placed the golden circlet around the ebony head. He turned, and could not escape.

He tried to climb from the grave, but sank to his knees. The king will not let me go, thought Davis. The dead will not let me live.

They are not finished. What more do they want from me?

But warm hands reached down for him, and friendly voices called his name.

His friends pulled him out of the darkness, onto the floor of the Minster.

Davis was weak, but Skip helped him to his feet.

"It's all right, then," said Skip. "He's going to be fine."

They were all silent, gazing into the grave. Irene ran to one of the candles, and hurried back with it. The dark tilted, and shifted around them as she approached.

"He is quiet now," said Irene.

The hands held the hilt. The head rolled slightly and the circlet crown rolled with it.

The body was still.

Davis could sense it. All over York the broken fragments of darkness dissolved. The thrashing spirit was asleep. And not only in the city. It was within him, too, this spreading, invisible light.

"May he rest in peace," breathed Langton.

For a moment no one could speak.

"Shall I bury him, then?" asked Skip.

32

Dr. Higg woke.

Davis and Langton were the first two faces to greet him. Langton had lost a good deal of weight, but looked quite fit. Davis looked the same as always, although he carried a pair of crutches.

Such dreams.

Time had slipped. He had lost days, he sensed. Longer.

He struggled to clear his mind. "You all have some sort of story to tell," said Higg. "You've been involved in some sort of mischief."

Even Langton, it seemed. That was very unlikely, and yet Langton had that hen-on-an-egg look about him. He had been involved in something, and now he felt smug about it.

Higg sat upright. He was very hungry. The strangest dreams. The blackened face before his that would not let him wake. The whisper in his ear.

All gone now. It was morning, and bright.

"Davis can tell you everything," said Langton. "There isn't really all that much to tell. You look well, William."

Davis did not know how much to tell him at once, although Dr. Hall had suggested that he was robust enough to take any amount of shock. His vital indicators were all quite sound, Dr. Hall

194

had reported. "The mystery is still irritating," he said. "But I'm always delighted to see a patient recover."

The hardest part would be the news about Jane. Her body had been found that very morning, bumping the landing near Lendal Bridge, miles from Bishopthorpe, and upriver. Whatever the children had seen in the water at Bishopthorpe, it had not been Jane, although perhaps the handbag they had found floating had inspired them to see the woman it had belonged to.

Davis was pleased that news of Mandy was, at last, good. She had been found wandering in a daze near Overton, several miles west of York. She had suffered a concussion, and had been confused about what had happened and where she was. A cow had, it seemed, awakened her by nudging her with what Mandy had described as "the dullest curiosity imaginable." She had suffered hypothermia and, it had been felt, the beginnings of pneumonia. She had stumbled into a farm owned by a local historian who had once studied medicine. He was a handsome, ruddy-faced widower, and he insisted on nursing Mandy himself at the farm. Davis had spoken to her on the telephone, and she had sounded delighted with life.

Peter would never know that the Skeldergate Man had been using him, all along, contriving to use Peter's skills to give him the power to walk.

"How is everyone?" asked Dr. Higg.

"Everyone is well," said Davis. "Almost everyone. There has been a little trouble."

Trouble. Higg hated the sound of that.

"How is the Skeldergate Man?"

"Resting comfortably."

Higg turned away. "I had one dream stranger than all the others. I dreamed that I was in a room with the Skeldergate Man. In the lab, where I was sitting up with him. And he moved. Moved, and turned his head." The memory made him look toward the daylight.

Davis and Langton did not speak.

"He turned his head," said Dr. Higg. "And he looked at me."

Late in the morning, after he had eaten, and after all the bad news imaginable had been fed to him along with the chicken pie, Dr. Higg got out of bed and sat in a chair. He wanted to be far from

York, far from this hospital room. He had always loved mornings in the Mediterranean for that really fierce light, the light that sweeps the Appian Way and makes a man wish he could live forever.

Such sorrow. Not disbelief. No, he believed it all.

Plain, undiluted sorrow. It was especially bitter news about Peter. He had been such a bright young man. He had been cremated yesterday.

Such bright young people. Such a waste.

Once he had found a jaw belonging to a Neanderthal, in the Dolomites, on a stormy summer afternoon. And he had stood there holding that crescent of bone, and felt that he was a part of something so wonderful he did not have to understand it. It simply was. And he was a treasure, for all his mortality, because he was human.

He would have to stop spending so much time remembering. He had work to do.

"That dream," said Dr. Higg. "That dream of the Skeldergate Man looking at me." Dr. Higg sighed. "That wasn't a dream, was it."

Davis made a smile, not quite sad—kind, really. He did not speak for a moment. "No," he answered at last. "It was not a dream."

Rain pattered against the window. Davis held Irene. It was late at night, perhaps even the next morning. They had awakened and made love, and now lay listening to the water chiming in the drainpipe.

Dr. Hall had pronounced Irene very lucky. Her scalp was only slightly lacerated. The human skull was strong, but the brain, Dr. Hall had said, was so much water. Irene could have been killed. As it was, she did not even need aspirin any longer.

"Once," said Irene, gazing into the dark, "I was going to be a physician. But the old things called to me. I wanted to know what happened long ago. Perhaps I wanted to give life to the dead." She was quiet for a moment. "I think of Jane."

Davis lay staring into the darkness he shared with her. "I know."

At last Irene asked, "Are you thinking of Jane, too?"

"I'm thinking of everyone. But Jane, too. What a terrible way to die."

"It is a world of terrible things, Davis. We live and we are sad some days and then some days we are happy."

The autopsy had been finished that afternoon. The police were saying nothing, because they were mystified. She had been strangled by having a foreign object, some weapon both long and supple, thrust down her throat. Like a length of leather. This was the second such death recently. The Skeldergate team would be questioned tomorrow. The police would be very unhappy with what they would hear, and, furthermore, they would not believe it.

"Do you suppose the police will want to dig up the Skeldergate Man?" asked Irene.

"I hope not."

"He will be an important witness."

"We will dissuade them."

"The Skeldergate Man needs a long rest. But what do police, or anyone else, know about death?"

The rain fell more heavily, a sound that filled Davis with peace.

Nothing, thought Davis. We all know nothing.

He held Irene in his arms, and slept.

This time the lake was still, and empty. There was no wind. The opposite shore was a dark line of land under a blank sky. He was alone. The water rippled, and then smoothed again, like writing erasing and unfolding itself.

No one walked the distant shore. There was only the sky and the water. He gazed across the empty lake, knowing that she would never come again.

And then there was nothing, only sleep, and the tireless promise of the rain.